# THE SUPERPOWER PROJECT

## PAUL BRISTOW

### ILLUSTRATED BY

## LUKE NEWELL

Kelpies

THE FISHING VILLAGE OF GREENOCK, 1772. DUSK.

A BLINDING FLASH DISTURBED THE EVENING!

GGGGZZZZZSPLOOOOSH

SOME COULD NOT RESIST SETTING OFF TO LOOK.

DON'T GO NEAR IT!

THEY FOUND ONLY DANGER.

CRAAAACKKK!

I CAN'T SEE THEM!

THE LIGHT FADED. THE RIVER CALMED.

SOMEHOW THEY HAD SURVIVED.

BUT LIFE WOULD NEVER BE THE SAME FOR THEM...

## CHAPTER 1...
## UP AND DOWN

There was something strange about the way Megan's gran had exploded. The strangeness wasn't that she was on holiday at the time; it wasn't that it was particularly unlucky because she had won the holiday in a competition; it wasn't even that she was water-skiing when it happened. No. It was that before exploding on faulty water-skis on her unexpected holiday, she had not phoned Megan when she said she would. Gran always phoned. Always.

Megan's mum suggested that it was 'maybe because of all the sangria', but still, it didn't feel right. None of it felt right. Everyone made a sad, understanding face when Megan said this, so she decided to stop talking about it.

Now, weeks later, she sat on her bed, holding a letter her gran had left for her. Megan brushed her dark hair out of her eyes and stared at the envelope some more, not quite ready to open it yet.

The week that followed the explosion had been very strange. Exploding on holiday is clearly quite an inconvenient thing to do; serious black-suited people kept turning up at the house with forms for Mum and Dad to fill in. Newspapers and a television crew wanted to speak to them as well, because it was such a 'tragic' and 'unusual' story. Megan was pretty sure her gran would have been delighted to be tragic and unusual.

Lots of people were big fans of Megan's gran's books, and sent emails, cards or flowers to say how sad they were at her death. Some even sent little cuddly knitted toys of her monsters. Mum really didn't know what to do with those; even though they were woollen, a few of them were still pretty terrifying. Gorskyn had always been Megan's favourite, so she took one to keep in her room. Its little tentacles had tassels on the end.

She had not been allowed to go to the funeral, because Dad said it would be too sad, which Megan sort of thought was the point. Even clown funerals must be sad. There were no understanding faces when she said this, though. She was certain Mum quietly phoned the doctor.

Instead, while everyone else went up to the hillside cemetery, Megan's great-aunt Gerty had taken her to a café in Gourock. The only good thing about this was that Megan had been allowed to take her best friend, Cameron, along too. Cam was slightly more interested in the selection of ice cream than in comforting Megan, but Megan was relieved to have something normal to do. It hadn't felt like a proper goodbye, especially because her aunt had refused to talk about Gran.

"Best not," she had said. "Your granny Sarah was a lovely lady, but a strange one. All that sad business when she was wee."

Megan stared at the envelope in her hand. It was from the stationery set she had made Gran for Christmas last year. It had taken ages, but she had made everything by hand, from the paper to the little wooden box it all came in. The letter smelled of Gran's perfume. The last time she'd smelled that perfume was on their pre-holiday walk round the dam, feeding the swans. Gran had said something Megan couldn't stop thinking about.

"Do you remember when I used to read you *The Ugly Duckling*?" asked Gran.

Megan nodded, hoping this wasn't her gran's attempt to start talking about growing up. "You always did a funny duck voice," she said.

"Well... it's a load of rubbish. People spend years waiting to be beautiful swans. What a waste of time. Just be a beautiful duck and get on with it." Gran had turned and grinned at Megan, but her grin had faded into a look Megan didn't recognise, before she quickly changed the subject. "Come on, you can help me pack – don't let me forget my Nintendo."

Megan had wanted to tell Gran her secret that day. She knew she would understand, know what to do.

It was too late to tell her now. All too late. All she had was the letter.

No one else was allowed to open or read it: "Your gran made it very clear that we must advise you to open the letter alone," the lawyer had said when she handed it over.

Now her parents were in bed and it was pitch-black outside, Megan knew it was time. She pulled at the envelope, carefully, as if it were full of diamonds and gunpowder. Inside was a very small piece of paper, some of the vellum parchment Megan had made by flattening out wood pulp.

*There can't be much written on that*, thought Megan, a little disappointed.

There were two other items in the envelope: a piece of old newspaper and one of those fold-out street maps of the town. For now, though, Megan was only interested in her letter. Sure enough, it was very short, but the first line said almost everything Megan hoped it would.

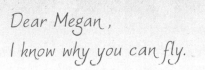

Dear Megan,
I know why you can fly.

CHAPTER 2...
HERE AND THERE

It was true. Megan could fly. Properly fly. Out of windows and up through clouds. It had started happening a few months ago – she had woken up with her nose squashed almost flat against her ceiling.

At first she thought there must have been an earthquake – there had been a few tremors earlier in the year – but then she realised everything else was still where it was supposed to be. Only she had moved. Megan spent a few moments not falling, and gently moving about by pushing her hands across the ceiling. Then she pushed away and floated, horizontal and happy in the middle of her room.

The best bit, the strangest bit, was how flying had been so easy to work out, how quickly she became good at it, like it was something she had always known how to do – not at all like riding a bike. When Megan was learning how to cycle, she had dented three cars, knocked over a shed and broken a leg. It wasn't even her own leg.

Megan continued reading her gran's beautiful old-fashioned handwriting:

I really want to be able to explain it all to you, but if you are reading this, it's because they finally caught up with me. I can't risk writing it all down. But Megan, I need you to find out for yourself. Follow the map. Then you'll know what you have to do.

All my love sweetheart. Fly safe.

Next, Megan carefully unfolded the map, laying it out on her bed. *Greenock, Port Glasgow and Gourock and Surrounding Environs 1953 Ordnance Survey*. Megan stared at the map, at street names and places she did not recognise, avenues and parkland from long ago. There were five numbered circles on the map. None of them in places she knew.

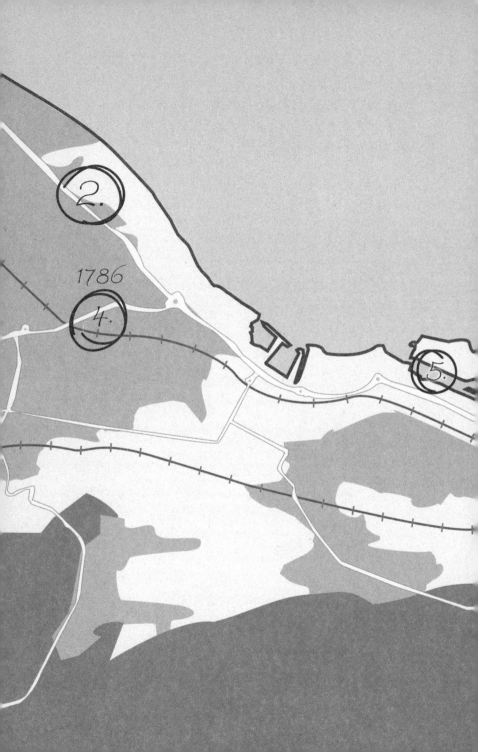

# GREENOCK, PORT GLASGOW

### and GOUROCK
### and SURROUNDING ENVIRONS
#### 1953 Ordnance Survey

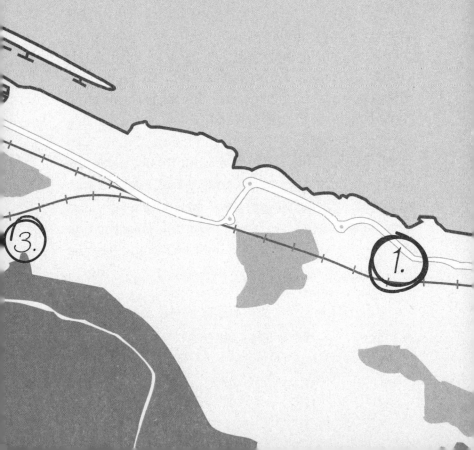

Number one was a hillside in Port Glasgow; number two down by the docks in Greenock. The circle for number three was marked beside what looked like a hospital, but it wasn't where the hospital was now. Four was a cemetery with the date 1786 scrawled above it in Gran's messy handwriting, and five was at the massive old sugar warehouses where they were building a new marina.

This was exactly the sort of thing her gran would do. She used to make treasure hunts for Megan all the time. Most grans just dished out sweeties; Megan's gran would write her strange rhyming clues and have her searching all over the house. The sweets always tasted better when she found them herself.

The best hunt was in the summer holidays a few years ago, when she had Megan searching all around the garden for clues. Each clue led to a trickier one, sending her through the bushes and behind the sunflowers, past where the goldfish were buried, until finally, under the garden shed she'd found the prize: a kite. Megan's gran had made it herself from green and purple silks and some old bamboo cane. It was beautiful. They went up into the hills behind the town for a picnic and flew the kite all afternoon.

*I wonder what she's hidden this time.*

The letter and the map made some sort of sense to Megan, but the newspaper page was a complete mystery. There was a story about a weird fish washing up from the river, an advert for Golden Syrup, and a photo of a scary-looking old building. She folded it back up and put it with the letter in her China-print keepsake box under her bedside cabinet. The map she put in her schoolbag.

Excited, she did her best to fall asleep, because unfortunately, none of those mysterious things were going to stop her having to go back to school tomorrow.

CHAPTER 3...

TIME AND PLACE

A pale thin man in a suit stood at the front of the class beside Miss McCue. He was completely bald, in that really shiny way, and the fact that you could see his whole head meant you could see how bumpy it was.

"Maybe he's got a really big brain or something," said Cam, not even all that quietly.

Cameron and Megan sat together in most classes and had done since Primary 1. Even then he was the tallest in class. He pretended he wasn't, though, always hunching up or curling in on himself, like some massive spindly legged spider constantly trying to hide under the nearest rock. Except there were no rocks big enough. Sometimes, when he said rude things far too loudly in class, Megan really wished there were.

"Right first year!" Miss McCue looked at Cam very briefly before beaming her award-winning smile across the class. "Today we have a real treat for you. Mr Finn is here from Waterworx, the people who are regenerating the old parts of town and building all the modern sculptures you've been looking at in art class. We've been given the opportunity to help design the next one! Isn't that great?"

Cam had his hand up, always a danger when a visitor came.

"Yes Cameron," said Miss McCue, looking like she was trying to send him a telepathic message along the lines of, *Please remember how upset that fireman got last time.*

"Are they going to pay us?" asked Cameron.

Miss McCue did her best charming laugh. "No Cam, we're helping design a sculpture because we'll all learn something and it will be good fun."

Cameron had his hand up again, even though Megan had just elbowed him.

"Yes Cameron," said Miss McCue through gritted teeth.

"It says in the paper Waterworx have millions and millions of pounds."

Miss McCue smiled nervously at Mr Finn, who thankfully seemed to be taking it all in his stride.

"That's actually true, Cameron," said Mr Finn, "but most of it is to spend on regenerating the town to make it better for everyone. I tell you what, though, I'll do you all a deal. You want to make a deal?"

The class perked up a bit, now there was a potential opportunity for free stuff.

"This is an old building you have here. Your head teacher was telling me you have a very leaky roof... is that right?"

Stacey's hand went up this time.

"Yes?" said Mr Finn.

"There was a big bulge in the ceiling in French class and it burst and all this water poured out onto Steven Barclay and there were drowned pigeons in it."

Everyone laughed.

"Dear me. Well, if you help us with a new sculpture, we'll make sure your leaky roof is no longer a problem. How does that sound?"

The class was unimpressed.

"And, of course, the person with the winning design will get a new Playstation," Mr Finn added quickly.

Result.

"Ok everyone," said Miss McCue quickly. "Mr Finn is going to take us to see one of the new sculptures being built at the shipyard in Port Glasgow. Yes Cameron?"

"How much can our sculpture cost? Can ours be made out of platinum?"

"No," said Miss McCue.

Megan and Cam sat in the middle of the bus, far enough away from the snogging at the back, but not near enough the front to be involved in rehearsing songs from the school show. It was the first time they had properly talked since the day of the funeral.

"Gran left me a letter."

"That's nice. My gran left us lots of out-of-date cat food and an old handbag full of raffle tickets."

"It had a map with it."

"I did get fifty quid, though, so I bought a new game," said Cam, drifting off.

"Cam, are you even listening?"

"A map. Your gran gave you a map."

"Yes. A map of round here. It's marked with numbers. I think she wanted me to find something."

"What? Treasure?" Cam laughed.

"I don't think so. This is something else, just for me."

"Right."

"And I want you to help me find it."

Megan saw a smile flicker briefly across Cameron's face. Right now, she wasn't totally sure how to get Cam to help her find the secret of why she could fly without actually telling him that she could fly. But she knew she could trust him and that she needed his help.

"Let's see it then," said Cameron.

Megan took the map out of her bag and unfolded it. "There are five places she's picked out. Number one is in Port Glasgow." Megan pointed to the tiny red circle. "I think I'm supposed to go to each place in order. That's the way her treasure hunts used to work."

Cam traced his long fingers across the streets. "This is

a really old map. Some of these places aren't there any more."

"But I bet you still know where to find them?"

"Maybe. I'm pretty sure that one is the old hospital, and that's the tobacco warehouses, which have been empty for years."

Megan smiled. "See. I knew you'd be able to do it. What's this one?"

"Behind the new flats in the ropeworks? It's just a supermarket I think. Wait..." Cam took out his phone. "Map app, I'm gonna save them all as locations," he explained and started tapping and swiping as the coach they were on pulled up outside the shipyard. Cam ignored everyone else undoing their seatbelts and filing off the coach as he stared from the map to his phone and back again. "The first one is really close! An old bomb shelter apparently."

Megan grinned.

"No," said Cam, "absolutely not. We're here to appreciate some rubbish art. I was grounded for a month after we got caught skidging last time."

"But how good were those monster trucks?"

"Cameron! Megan! We haven't got all day!" Miss McCue called from outside.

# CHAPTER 4...
# LOST AND FOUND

Mr Finn led them into a big warehouse. There were bits of scaffolding and old boats in the far corner, and random traffic cones were scattered around, presumably warning about some unseen health-and-safety issue. In the centre of the warehouse was an enormous metal egg. Mr Finn was pointing at it, looking very proud.

"This sculpture is called Phoenix Egg. It's going in the new town square beside our offices. Can anyone guess why we've chosen the name Phoenix Egg?"

"Do you really like eggs?" asked Scott Malcolm.

"I do really like eggs," said Mr Finn, "but that's not the reason."

"Could you just not think of anything better?" asked Cam.

Mr Finn was a very quick learner, so he was already ignoring Cam. "The sculpture represents rebirth and the future of the town," he said, "because a Phoenix rises from the ashes to live again." He paused dramatically, as if he was waiting for a round of applause.

"Our town hasn't been burnt to ashes though," said Megan.

"No," smiled Mr Finn. "Of course it hasn't. Shall we take a closer look at the sculpture?"

Cam took out his phone.

"Sorry," said Mr Finn, "no photos yet. We don't want to spoil the surprise for everyone."

"It's for my collection," said Cam. "I took photos of the other ones."

"Really?" said Mr Finn, unsure whether Cam was being truthful or rude – or both. "Which is your favourite?"

"I like the round one near the old dam," said Cam.

"Evolve," said Mr Finn, making it sound more like an instruction than a name. "What do you like about that one?"

Miss McCue had zeroed in on their conversation and was now hovering nearby waiting to calm things down when Cam said something cheeky. It would only be a matter of time.

"I like how curved all the bits are," said Cam. "It's like a hollow snowman that's fallen over or something."

Megan was probably the only person who could tell that this was genuinely heartfelt appreciation from Cam. He did actually like that statue; they sat on it all the time.

"Perhaps you could tell the class more about the other sculptures, Mr Finn," said Miss McCue.

"Well, we've all heard that Evolve is Cameron's favourite," said Mr Finn. "And you can see Phoenix Egg here, but does anyone know about the others?"

"There's Resilience," said Cam, ignoring looks from both Megan and Miss McCue. "It's all jaggy. Don't like that one."

"I will be sure to pass that on to our designer, Cameron," said Mr Finn. "Can *anyone else* think of the other sculpture?" Mr Finn squinted towards the back of the class. "Yes. You. I didn't see you there."

"Come on! Speak up Kevin!" said Miss McCue.

"It's the one down near the college that looks like a giant with a clock for a face."

"Don't like that one either," said Cam. "Gives me the creeps."

"Yes, that one is called Chronos," said Mr Finn, attempting to speak over Cam. "Those are our four, but *you're* going to design the fifth and final sculpture."

Led by Mr Finn, the class wandered off towards the other sheds. Megan put her hand on Cam's shoulder to hold him back and pointed outside into the grey morning rain.

"So you think that's the spot Gran marked on the map, over there?" she whispered.

There was a steep slope just visible behind the supermarket, entirely covered in untidy bushes and trees.

"Pretty sure. I'll double-check." Cam rifled through his pockets for his phone. "Not here! I must have dropped it back when I took a photo of the egg."

"Cam! You're so careless with that phone," said Megan.

"It's fine."

"It's not fine! Normal phones aren't wrapped up in Sellotape to stop them falling to pieces!"

"Extra padding when I do drop it though," said Cam.

The rest of the class were still wandering round the yard listening to Mr Finn.

"Come on then," said Megan, "before someone notices."

The lights were all out in the warehouse now, making it more difficult to find phones or avoid industrial accidents. Megan and Cam tiptoed through the shadows towards the sculpture, careful not to stand or slip on anything that looked dangerous.

"Here it is," said Cam, picking up his phone, dusting it off and pushing the cracked screen to check it still worked.

"Shh!" said Megan. "What's that?"

"What's what?"

There was a tapping and hissing from inside the egg.

"Can you hear that too?" asked Megan.

"Uhhm. Yeah," said Cam. "Let's go."

Then the tapping got louder, more urgent, and between tiny gaps in the riveted plates, they could see a red glow, more obvious now in the darkness. It was as if there was something inside the metal egg, waiting to come out.

The lights flickered back on, silencing the tapping instantly. Startled, Megan and Cam turned to see Mr Finn at the doorway, staring.

"Your class is leaving," he said, "you'd better catch them up."

"Dropped my phone," said Cam, waving it by way of explanation.

"Yes. You should really be more careful."

Mr Finn stood motionless, waiting for them to leave. Both of them were only too happy to get out of his way.

PHOENIX EGG

CHAPTER 5...
DARK AND DANK

It took Megan all day to convince Cam that following the map into the old bomb shelter behind the supermarket was a good idea. Probably because it wasn't a good idea. It was a terrible idea. A terrible idea with a very good chance of rats.

"Hah! You aren't scared of rats are you Cam?" she'd said, not even fooling herself.

"No. I'm scared of the Black Death and Lyme disease."

Megan had to google that. It was pretty scary. So many scabs.

Eventually she gave up trying to convince him and announced she would go alone. That's when he agreed to come. Megan made a mental note to remember that for next time.

The old bomb shelter was a series of interconnected tunnels hollowed out under a cliff. Cam said it ran down underground for miles. Officially, of course, it was now considered a hazard, all blocked off and locked up. Unofficially, you could squeeze in behind the dodgy garages.

Cam was tucking his waterproof trousers into his welly boots for the third time.

"Cam, honestly, you're fine."

"What about leeches?"

"I don't think you get leeches here. Or piranha."

"You might. No one's been down here for years. It's an undisturbed ecosystem. Anything could be living there."

"Velociraptors under Port Glasgow?"

"No. But there's that big cat people are always seeing on the hills behind the town."

"And with miles of moorland to run across, it lives behind a supermarket? An urban puma?"

"Puma, velociraptor, piranha... whatever eats me, you'll have my mum to deal with."

Megan was actually a bit scared of Cam's mum – she was a nurse and not really one for nonsense. One time she found out he'd been trading all the fruit in his packed lunch for chocolate and Haribo and he was only allowed to eat raw vegetables and porridge for the rest of the month. That had been a really tough month for everyone.

"Ok? Ready to go?"

Cam nodded glumly.

The two waded into the darkness. The water was deeper than Megan had thought it would be, and she was starting to wish they hadn't bought their torches in the pound shop.

Megan stopped suddenly and gestured for Cam to stop too. "Shh. What's that?"

A distant splash echoed through the empty dark. Then another. And another. The unmistakable splish-splash of something else, walking through the tunnels towards them.

Cam looked around, trying to get his bearings. "Which way is that coming from?" Megan shushed him again.

More splashing, faster now, and nearer.

Cam reached for Megan, taking her hand to run back the way they had come.

"No it's *coming* from that way. Go this way!" hissed Megan.

Cam turned his torch towards the nearest junction in the tunnels: two eyes beamed eerily back at them, reflecting the faded torchlight. Megan and Cam both screamed as the creature splashed quickly towards them, its startled eyes dancing ever closer through the black. In a moment, the terrified deer had run past them both and back out into the streets above.

Cam was still screaming long after it had gone.

"Cam? Cam it's away now. It was just a deer."

"Did you see those eyes? It looked evil." Cam fumbled through his pockets, finally producing a packet of chewing gum. "Evil."

The two friends stood in silence for a moment.

"See," said Cam, "there *could* be a puma down here."

"Maybe that's why the deer was running," said Meg. It was supposed to be a joke, but it was too soon.

"Can we go yet?" Cam scowled.

"Just five more minutes. My gran wanted me to come down here. I'd really like to know why."

Steadying one another as they went, they wandered through what felt like miles of tunnels: past the rotted bench and bed frames where families must have huddled together as the bombs fell; past the tiny cubicles people used as toilets, and down towards the huge machines which stood at the tunnels' end.

"What are these?"

"Maybe for air conditioning. Or water pumps?"

The torchlight suddenly illuminated a face amongst the rust. Startled, Megan stumbled back into Cam.

"Look at this!"

It was a figure, a person, sculpted and built from metal. The head was a near perfect sphere, studded with rivets. Two eyes, large round bolts, stared vacantly into the shelter, and a wide rectangular gap, like a broken letterbox, was the figure's mouth. It hung open as if in surprise, or perhaps silently screaming.

"Cam, it's... it looks like a robot."

In the low light of their pound-shop torches, steel still gleamed through all the grease and dirt.

"What do you think it's doing down here?" said Cam.

"I've no idea. Looks like it's been here a long time though. This must be what Gran wanted me to find."

"But how did she know it was here? Did she build it, do you think?"

"Doubt it. She couldn't even do Lego."

Cam tapped it gently with his torch. "It's a bit rusty."

Megan was searching all around the robot for anything that looked important. "Hey, check this out, there's a button on his neck."

"Don't push it!" shouted Cam. "You could get a shock or something."

"Too late," said Megan, pushing it anyway, and then jumping back a bit just in case.

Nothing.

Cam hit it with his torch again. "Oh well."

At once, the robot's eyes flared an angry orange and it grabbed Cam's arm. "Unnnnnderaaaaaattack. Ehhhhhnnnehmeee."

"Run!" shouted Megan.

# CHAPTER 6...

# MUCK AND BRASS

"I can't run, it's got my arm!" shouted Cam, pointing to his arm as if proof was required.

"Let him go!" shouted Megan, which she knew was a bit of a long shot.

The robot immediately released its grip on Cam's arm and turned to look at Megan, eyes lighting up.

"Zeeraah."

"Maybe that's its space name or something," suggested Cam, rubbing his rapidly bruising arm.

"Wherry zerah?"

"Pardon?"

The lights in the robot's eyes flashed on and off in what felt like mild frustration. "Wherr ee zerahh?"

"Is that Spanish, Cam?"

"Not sure."

"Well you're the one who's supposed to be learning it."

"Where izz zerahh?"

Megan felt a bit sorry for the robot. She was sure if it could have managed another facial expression, it would have gone for exasperated.

"Serrah."

"Wait... Sarah? Sarah my gran? Sarah Stone?"

Eyelights flashed. "Sarah Stone. Aye amfur Sarah Stone."

"Your gran had a robot? How cool is that?" said Cam.

"I'm Megan Stone," said Megan, smiling. "Sarah's my gran."

"Take. Me. To. Sarah."

Cam shuffled uncomfortably.

"I... I can't," said Megan. "She... just died a few weeks ago."

The robot's lights flickered silently, there were a series of clicks and whirring noises.

Megan instinctively touched the robot's cold metal arm. "How did you know my gran? I mean, she was always a bit funny, but having a robot seems odd even for her."

"Sarah Stone."

"Yes, how did you know Sarah?"

"Protect."

"Like a bodyguard? Protect her from what?"

"What? Yes. What."

"Don't be daft Megan, your gran didn't need a bodyguard. I saw her in the Post Office that time a guy tried to jump the queue. He ended up actually crying."

"Well she must have used the robot for something –

I mean why would Gran send me down here to look for it otherwise?" Megan turned to the robot and asked, "Why are you here?"

The robot leaned forward to look at Megan properly and its eyes brightened. "You. Look. Sarah."

Megan sighed. Everyone always said they looked alike. It seemed like most questions were too tricky for the robot, so she decided to try something simpler. "Do you have a name?"

"Aye haf forgot."

"Forgotten."

The robot's eyes flickered again, like light bulbs before a power cut. It tapped the back of its head as if trying to knock the memory back into place.

Cam looked at his watch. "Well, this was weird, but shouldn't we be getting home now?"

"We can't leave him here," said Megan, taking the robot's hand.

"*It*," said Cam, "we can't leave *it* here. And yes we can. Come on, before something horrible down here wakes up feeling hungry."

Megan stared at Cam very severely, so severely that Cam jumped back just a tiny bit.

"Cam, seriously. My gran left me a robot. I'm not leaving it rusting down a tunnel."

Cam had seen this look before. It was the look that usually meant he was just about to be wrong. "Megan, think about it. Where will it go?"

"In your spare room?"

"All Mum's keep-fit stuff is packed away in there," protested Cam. "You never know, she might actually go in and use it or something."

"Well he can't stay here."

A crackling beep echoed around the tunnel. Then another, shorter this time.

"Do you hear that? It's a bomb. Megan, it's a bomb, let's go!"

The robot once again grabbed Cam's arm, stopping him from running away.

"It's got me! Megan, it's got me. We're going to explode!" Cam struggled, trying to pull his arm free. "Get it off me! Megan, get it off me!"

"Stop it!" said Megan, which, to be fair, could have applied to either the robot or Cam. "That's enough. Both of you."

The robot stared at Megan, and gently released Cam's arm. "I... sorry," he said. "I did not want you to leave."

Megan nodded. "I understand, but just to check, what is the beeping?"

"I am not a bomb."

"That's exactly what a bomb would say," said Cam, still rubbing his arm. "Let's go."

"Wait," said the robot. Slowly, he opened a rusted grille in his chest. Inside was a small machine, with springs and several buttons positioned around a large lever that ran from one end to the other. Wires ran up into the robot's head. As the beeping echoed again, the lever moved sharply.

"That's... I think that's a Morse-code machine," said Cam, who did occasionally pay attention in science in case someone showed them how to do controlled explosions.

"A what?" said Megan, staring inside the robot.

"Morse-code machine. They used them for sending messages, especially secret ones during the war."

"Oh yeah," said Megan, "dot dash dot and all that. Why is it beeping?"

The robot's eyes flashed again. "I am receiving a message."

There were a further series of beeps, and now also clicks.

"Who from?" asked Cam.

"There are five. Stone is one."

"Stone?" asked Megan. "My gran Sarah Stone is one? Only five what?"

"Only five send messages. Sarah Stone is one of five."

"My gran could send you messages?"

The robot nodded creakily. "Once. Ago."

"Did she leave a message for me?"

"I cannot know. I'm forgotten."

Cam was peering inside the robot's chest cavity, tapping on the machine. "There's nothing for it to print onto, all the paper has rotted."

"Could you figure it out?" asked Megan.

"I could maybe look it up online. But not in here. No signal."

"So he'll have to come with us?"

The robot squeakily nodded his approval once again and slowly began to move forward from the wall.

"He's attached! He's tied to the wall," said Megan, horrified.

The robot dragged himself forward, eyes flashing blankly as he pulled the wires from the wall, brickwork crumbling behind him.

"Fine!" said Cam. "Fine then. But can we just go before the rest of the tunnel falls down?"

# CHAPTER 7...
# LAW AND ORDER

Cam peered out of the bomb shelter into the dark early evening. "Right, it looks pretty clear. Come on, let's just stay off the radar."

"Radar?" The robot stopped suddenly, reached behind his ear and flicked a switch. "I am now invisible to radar."

"Excellent," said Cam, "that'll come in really handy if any submarines are looking for us."

The robot stopped. "Is the submarine back?"

"Cam, stop confusing him!" said Megan. "We're fine. He means we should try not to be seen."

"He should say what he means," observed the robot, with just the slightest note of irritation.

"Yes. He really should." Megan grinned. "Look, if anyone sees him we can just pretend he's our art homework or something we're building in IT," she added. "I mean no one's going to think he's an actual robot, are they?"

Cam stared again at the rusted and muck-caked figure, shambling squeakily out of the tunnel. "Well, certainly no one who thinks robots are cool, no."

The robot walked timidly forwards, creaking like an old garden gate. He looked around confused, as if trying to discover the source of the noise. Cam shook his head.

"I suppose he can't just be seen walking about though," said Megan. "We'll have to carry him."

"What? Are you joking? The whole way back to town?" said Cam.

"That would be... nice," said the robot. "I am very stiff after all this time."

Megan grabbed the robot's shoulders while Cam began lifting the legs.

"Have you got, like, an anti-gravity setting or something?" groaned Cam.

"Wait." The robot opened his chest panel and pulled a lever. "Try now."

Cam dragged up the robot's legs. "Nope! You weigh a ton!"

"Megan seems to be lifting with ease," said the robot.

"We'll just stop when we get too tired," said Megan, smiling.

Megan, Cam and the robot picked their way through the supermarket car park that hid the entrance to the bomb shelter.

"Do you know who built you?" Cam asked, when they stopped to rest.

The robot clicked and whirred once again. "What."

"Who. Built. You?" said Cam.

"The engineer. What."

"Ok. That narrows it down," said Cam.

"Was it someone from Waterworx?" tried Megan, thinking of the Phoenix Egg in the shipyard.

"I was built in 1809."

"Rubbish!" said Cam. "That's over two hundred years ago. They couldn't build robots like you in the olden days. Plus, you would have rusted away to nothing."

"There have been... replacement parts. Wars. But Mr Watt did not build me for war..."

"Mr Watt... wait... James Watt? James Watt the inventor?" asked Megan.

The robot tapped the back of his neck to indicate the sign welded there. Right where he had been smacking himself earlier. Letters and numbers were engraved across the old metal plate.

"Oh yeah! It says 'James Watt' right here," said Cam.

"You know Mr Watt?" the robot asked.

"Well, he's quite famous," explained Megan.

"I am named after him... Jimmy. A Tin Jimmy. TJ zero one."

"Tin Jimmy," smiled Megan, "nice to meet you. Now TJ, please can you tell us why my gran – Sarah Stone – wanted us to meet? Did you know her?"

TJ whirred and his eyes flickered for a moment. "There were cranes. And boats," he pointed to the riverside, "all along there."

Megan nodded. "Sounds like it's been a while then. There haven't been cranes here for decades." She placed a hand on his tin shoulder. "Can you remember why she wanted me to find you?"

"And why were you tied up in a bomb shelter anyway?" asked Cam, who clearly didn't believe in mollycoddling robots.

The robot, as if suddenly aware of his arms, moved them around. They squeaked horribly. "I was hiding."

"From what? Did Gran hide you?" asked Megan.

TJ clicked and whirred. Megan had started to realise this meant she wasn't going to get an answer. She gave him a reassuring pat on the back. "It doesn't matter just now."

"Yes it does!" said Cam. "Supposing whoever it's hiding from is now after u–?"

"I have been underground since 11:27 pm, 23 May 1965," TJ interrupted Cam.

There was a stunned silence. Once again, Megan could sense TJ's bewilderment through his robotic lack of expression.

"You've really been down a hole in the ground for *fifty years*?" asked Cam.

"How are you still working?" said Megan.

"Conserved battery power. I will need to recharge soon or I will stop moving."

"Cam's a bit like that with chocolate biscuits," said Megan.

Again, the robot stared into the dark, as if searching for something he could recognise. "Where are we going?" he asked.

"Good question," said Cam. "Megan invited you to my house. She's very kind like that."

"Cam, if not the spare room, you've got a shed we can hide him in! Where would he go in my house?"

Megan and Cam were so busy with their discussion that it took them a moment to realise they were no longer alone. TJ was standing perfectly still, being examined by two policemen.

"Very impressive," said the taller policeman of the two. "I'm assuming this is yours, yes?"

"It's an art project," explained Megan, "we're doing sculptures at school."

"Lots of sculptures round here just now," said the smaller policeman. "I like that one with all the pointy bits."

"Resilience," said Cam, shuddering.

"That's the one," said the small policeman. "And this is your effort then?"

"Yes," said Cam, "we were trying to work out how to move it."

"It's a bit late to be taking it for a walk," said the tall policeman.

"Yes, we're bringing it back from our friend's house," said Megan, feeling just a little bit bad about how easily that lie had happened, but generally quite pleased about how plausible it sounded.

"And I take it you didn't realise how heavy it was going to be," said the small policeman.

"No, we did," said Megan, "it's just that Cam hasn't really been trying very hard."

Cam glared at her as both the policemen shook their heads disapprovingly.

"It's getting dark," said the tall policeman. "I'd rather we got you and your art project home before you all get into trouble."

"Just to be clear though," said Cam, "we're not actually in trouble at the moment?"

"Not yet," said the small policeman, smiling.

"It's just that my mum's a nurse," said Cam, as if this explained everything. Or indeed anything.

Megan bundled into the back seat of the police car, arms outstretched to catch the robot, or any bits that might fall off him. Both policemen and Cam lifted TJ, pushing him towards the doors and into the back seat. His legs were still hanging out the other side.

"Just need to fold it up a bit," said the tall policeman, grunting with effort.

"Careful!" said Megan.

With a terribly unpleasant shriek, TJ's legs folded at the knee. The flakes of rust and clay that crumbled off them suggested it had been a long time since TJ had done squat jumps. He was folded, though, and inside the car.

"Don't forget seatbelts," said the tall policeman.

It was a short drive to Cam's house, and the policemen

were nice and chatty on the way, talking them through various recent crime statistics and their favourite types of biscuit. They even helped get TJ out of the car and into the garden shed, only banging his head on the door twice.

Smiling, they drove off.

"TJ are you ok?" said Megan, genuinely upset. "Did we break anything? Can you still move?"

There was a brief silence, then the already familiar clicks and whirrs.

"I am fine," said TJ, "though I think my kneecap may still be in the car."

# 8. SOUND AND FURY

There was a strange high-pitched howling, a piercing shriek that shattered the silence of the early evening and suggested unspeakable horror was nearby. Startled birds flew off into the sky, dogs barked, babies burst into tears. And in Mr Finn's house, one of the windows cracked and a teacup fell over.

"Haha!" Mr Finn was so pleased he was almost jumping up and down. "Finally! Victory for the Chaos Trumpet!" But before he had finished celebrating, all the brass buttons fell off the top, and two of the pipes popped with a defeated wheeze. "Nooo!" he shouted, hurling the trumpet across the laboratory, where it bounced off a rubber skeleton and into a big bin full of broken ray guns.

Mr Finn stopped and did some deep breathing, because that's what his doctor had told him to do when he got too angry. Right before Mr Finn disintegrated him with a ray gun. Inventing was supposed to be his way to relax. When he wasn't gritting his teeth being polite to annoying schoolchildren or shouting at Waterworx employees, Mr Finn liked to spend time turning useful household devices into dangerous weaponry. The Salsascope, the Microwump, the Smogmatronic – all really helpful for completing a variety of chores while destroying enemies.

Mr Finn just could not understand why his genius had gone unrecognised. How could that little twerp think his remarkable Resilience sculpture was 'jaggy'? Soon, though, everyone would know his name.

Mr Finn's laboratory was hidden beneath his huge house on the Esplanade, one of the few old parts of the town that had not been knocked down, mostly because it had all the really expensive houses in it. The big bay windows in these miniature mansions overlooked the river and the hills beyond.

Every night for the last three months, ever since he had arrived in town with Waterworx, Mr Finn had come to the lab and continued working on his creations. Then, at eight o'clock, he would stop to patiently push the buttons on his father's old Morse-code machine. Then he would wait to see if anything happened. Nothing ever did.

Tonight, though, the machine answered back.

Mr Finn was so surprised that he almost spilled his Earl Grey tea all over his radiation suit.

The code he received was gibberish, just random letters. But it was working, and that could only mean one thing.

"Someone has reactivated TJ01," said Mr Finn. "Finally!"

Mr Finn allowed himself a little smile, mostly because no one was there to see it.

"Now we can really get started."

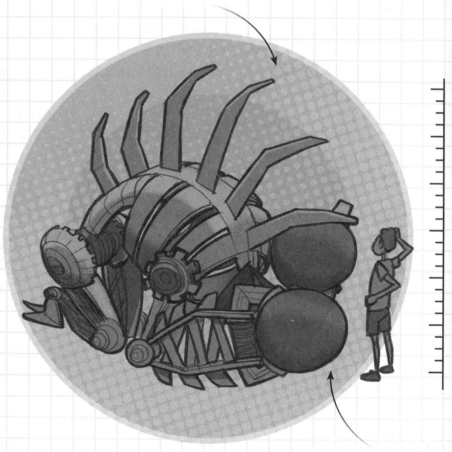

Jaggy enough?
Limited potential for
accidents.

The best solution
in case there's
any trouble.

RESILIENCE

# CHAPTER 9...

## CODE AND THEORY

Miss McCue beamed at the class. Not a sunbeam, warm and pleasant, more a sort of laser beam, precise and piercing. "Today we begin researching and designing our very own statue for Waterworx."

Cam groaned inwardly.

"Cam! No complaining."

Startled, Cam turned to Meg. "Did that happen out loud?"

"They always happen out loud, Cam," said Megan.

"Our sculpture will be near the old sugar warehouses."

Meg and Cam exchanged glances. Those warehouses were circled on Gran's map; this might be worthwhile after all.

"Maybe the statue could be a big sugar cube?" said Garry.

"Maybe!" said Miss McCue enthusiastically, even though this was a totally rubbish idea.

"Could it be a big bag of sugar beside a teacup and spoon?" asked Gemma, expanding on the theme but still essentially being rubbish.

"It could be almost anything," said Miss McCue. "Now off you go in your pairs to the IT suite where Miss McTeer will show you how to use proper online archives."

Miss McCue had deliberately not paired Cam and Megan together for this project. Probably because the last time they worked as a pair, the school had to be evacuated. There was no firm evidence that Cam and Megan were to blame, but they had laughed about it a lot more than everyone else.

Cam had been paired with a really quiet boy from class, Kevin McCallum. Cam didn't like Kevin. It's not that there was anything really unpleasant about him, it was just that Cam didn't like most people. Especially people he didn't know. He knew this was a bad habit and he was trying to grow out of it. He just wasn't trying very hard.

Kevin was one of those pupils who sort of faded into the background, like wallpaper. Always there, but never noticeably so. If he ever committed a crime, he would almost certainly get away with it because the police description would be: 'An average boy of average height and build with no distinguishing features.'

Kevin tapped Cam on the shoulder. "I was thinking the statue could be a big Licquorice Allsorts man, because, you know, sugar."

Cam smiled in spite of himself. "Yeah. Or a sherbet fountain that actual sherbet comes out of."

"Can't be any worse than a sugar cube," said Kevin. "I've got quite a few different ideas for what we could do. Would you like to see?"

"Yes Kevin," said Cam, hoping that Kevin was one of those partners who liked to do all the work. "I really would."

On the other side of the classroom, Megan was partnered with Gemma, who was busy giggling and googling tea-party pictures for inspiration.

Megan's mind was still on TJ and the map, however. She had barely slept the night before – whenever she dropped off she had insane dreams about flying away from explosions, TJ creaking and flickering, and Gran drawing circles on a map and telling her something she could never properly hear. Her arms were bruised from accidentally floating into objects in her room.

She wondered if TJ would ever remember what her gran had meant for her to do with him. They'd plugged him into an extension cable and left him charging in Cam's shed. Maybe he'd remember more when he was fully powered, or maybe they'd find something to fix him with at the next location on the map?

As her eyes wandered around the IT class, she spotted

a bundle of coloured cables attached to a Lego model of a crane. Miss McTeer was busily footering with the cables, and every few minutes she would turn to a nearby computer screen, type something on the keyboard, and watch while the crane slowly moved. Sometimes the movements seemed to make her happy, other times, she would scowl, tweak the cables and type in something else.

"Bored with research already?" said Miss McTeer when she realised she was being watched. But she was smiling, because she was one of the three nice teachers all schools are legally obliged to have.

"Well," said Megan carefully, "what you're doing looks a bit more interesting."

Miss McTeer nodded the grateful nod of the under-appreciated, and Megan knew she wouldn't have to worry about research for the rest of the afternoon. "Would you like me to explain what I'm trying to build?"

"Totally," said Megan.

"Well, I've spent the morning hooking all these cables up between the Lego and my computer. Now I'm programming the Lego to move."

Megan delicately picked up a tiny green plastic circuit board. "What does this bit do?"

Miss McTeer smiled. "That's the brains of the operation. It's the computer that controls the whole set-up."

Megan looked again at the small plastic wafer. "This thing?"

"Yep. It's called a Goozberri Five," said Miss McTeer. "It's a really powerful wee computer that can pretty much be connected to anything. Once I've tested the program out on the Lego, I'm going to use it to control a robotic arm."

Now Megan really was interested. "Where did you get a robotic arm?"

"I made it at home," said Miss McTeer.

"That's amazing," laughed Megan.

"Is it?" said Miss McTeer, who probably wasn't used to people thinking that sort of thing was at all amazing. "Listen, I've started a lunchtime coding club for second years. You should come along if you're interested. Everyone's doing their own project."

"Really?" said Megan, surprised to find she was actually excited by the idea.

"Yeah! You could have a go at programming anything you like. Some of my pupils are making alarms for their rooms, or weather stations for geography homework, even connecting them to solar panels. It's really up to you!"

"Hmm," said Megan, "I think I have something I'd like to program."

It had been a while since Megan and Cam had walked home from school having enjoyed their day. It was quite a pleasant experience.

"What's Kevin like then?" said Megan. "He always seems really quiet."

"A good laugh actually. He gets a bit overexcited about stuff," said Cam. "Think we might suggest the statue is one of your gran's monsters."

"Aw Cam," said Megan, "Gran would've loved that."

Cam smiled and they walked in silence for a moment.

"I'm joining Miss McTeer's coding club," said Megan. "I'm going to learn how to program TJ."

"Coding club?" said Cam. "That sounds even less fun than the chess club."

Megan punched Cam on the arm. "Don't you get it? I can program in school, pretend it's for a Lego robot or something, then see if I can connect it to TJ."

"But he's already programmed. Won't that just confuse him?" asked Cam, for once sounding mildly concerned about the robot.

Megan smiled. "You said 'him'. TJ must be growing on you."

Cam groaned.

"His programming has to be a bit old-fashioned," Megan continued. "But we might as well try to help him remember stuff."

"Maybe," said Cam. "It would just be a shame to accidentally turn him into a terminator or something. Oh, I meant to say, think I found a place online that does Morse-code paper."

"Really?"

"Yeah, for museums and science classes. I asked Mum to order some for us."

"That's brilliant Cam!"

Cam stopped outside his garden gate. "Yeah, it's given me an excuse for all the strange lights and noises in the shed while we've been oiling and charging TJ," he explained. "I've told her I'm using it as a lab."

Just then, there was a small but very definite *boom*, causing the two of them to jump. Megan briefly forgot to land back on the ground after her jump, but fortunately Cam was too busy looking in disbelief at his garden shed. Smoke billowed out from beneath its door and through both–now broken–windows. The door creaked open and they could see TJ standing inside with a smoking bottle of fertilizer. The beeping sound of the Morse-code machine echoed round the garden.

"Cameron," said TJ calmly, "your shed is compromised. I may need somewhere else to hide."

"What have you done?" shouted Cam.

"It is not my fault," said TJ. "The contents of the shed are dangerous if mixed together and set on fire. There should be a sign explaining the danger, Cameron."

Cam groaned. "This is going to be worse than when I bought bath bombs for the goldfish."

"Is your mum in?" asked Megan, genuinely worried.

"She's on backshift," said Cam, "but my dad'll be in." He glanced nervously up at the house.

"Look," said Megan, "I'll take some of the blame. We can say it was a science project that went wrong."

Cam looked at the smoking hollow shell that used to

be a shed. "I suppose if they think I was doing school work I might only lose one month's pocket money."

"Cam? What's this? What's going on?" Cam's dad was hanging out the window, looking tired and unhappy.

"We're ok Mr Molloy," said Megan quickly, "but I think we copied down the chemistry homework wrong."

Cam's dad looked at the smoking garden shed. "Cameron, what have we told you about paying attention in class?" he barked.

"Sorry Dad."

"Get it cleaned up," he said. "You can explain it to your mum. And what's that?" He pointed down to TJ.

"Art project," said Megan. "We're doing sculptures."

"Flippin' sculptures everywhere," muttered Cam's dad, disappearing back behind the curtains. "Stupid Chronos bell always making me jump out of my skin at work..."

"There," said Megan, turning back to Cam. "All sorted."

"Oh, you think?" said Cam, scowling at TJ.

"None of this would have happened if there had been a danger sign, Cameron," said TJ.

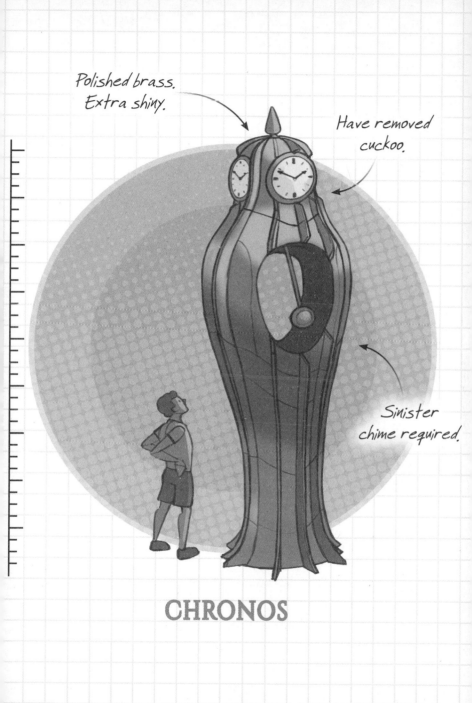

Polished brass.
Extra shiny.

Have removed
cuckoo.

Sinister
chime required.

CHRONOS

CHAPTER 10...

BRICKS AND MORTAR

Even if Cam hadn't just lost his next month's pocket money, it was pretty clear to Megan that Tin Jimmy would no longer be welcome at his house. It was time for a flit.

This time Megan and Cam decided to move TJ using a wheelbarrow. But after a few minutes of pushing, Megan was hoping for another lift from the police.

"This is heavier," said Cam. "How can it be heavier?"

"At least it has wheels," said Megan.

"Would it help if I used my wheels?" asked TJ.

"Your wheels?" asked Megan.

A pair of ancient-looking roller skates popped out of the robot's feet.

"You have wheels!" shouted Cam. "Why didn't you say that before we started carrying you round like a king?"

TJ clicked. "It did not seem important."

"Cam, honestly, a roller-skating robot would probably

have attracted even more attention."

TJ's wheels clunked back in.

"Where are we taking him anyway?" scowled Cam. "Somewhere he can't blow anything up, I hope."

"You know number two on Gran's map marks the old tobacco warehouses, down by the dock? I thought maybe we could leave him there when we check them out," suggested Megan. "You said they were lying empty."

"Yeah..." said Cam, "but I thought they were getting knocked down."

"Even more reason to search the place soon then."

Cam made the new face he had for whenever Megan talked about the map. It was supposed to make him look interested and pleased that they might be going somewhere dangerous, but it just looked like he had a dodgy tummy.

"It'll do for now anyway. Won't it TJ?" said Megan.

"It sounds better than the hazardous shed," said TJ.

"The shed was fine before you moved in," said Cam.

The old tobacco warehouses were just hollow shells in the truest sense. Going inside one was like being on a film set where the buildings are really just the front bit held up with wooden beams. Although each one had four sides and a roof, there was nothing left inside but broken glass, rubble and some very well-established pigeon colonies.

Megan, Cam and TJ stared through the grimy framework, collapsed fire escapes and missing floors. Now they were out of sight, TJ was free to move about on his own. His joints were much less noisy now Cam and Megan had oiled and cleaned him, and he was fully charged.

"Ehm… will you be ok here for a few nights TJ? Just until we find something better?" Megan felt a bit guilty about how they had 'rescued' him by moving him from a dank tunnel to a flimsy shed to a rotting warehouse.

"There are a lot of pigeons," observed TJ. "Can I have an umbrella?"

"Honestly, it won't be for long." Megan glanced over at Cam, hoping he would chip in with something positive and reassuring. He just looked horrified.

"Why would Gran want me to come here?" mused Megan.

"Why would *anyone* want to come here?" said Cam. "It's even worse than the gym hall."

Some pigeons flew between the beams above, scattering the intruders with old brick dust and dried pigeon poo.

"Any ideas TJ?" said Megan. "Do you remember ever coming here with Gran? It doesn't really seem like her sort of place."

"I do not recognise this building," said TJ, staring up towards the sky through the gaps in the roof.

"I suppose we'd better start looking then," said Megan. "I just wish I knew what we were looking for. Is there gonna be a robot at every place on the map?"

"If it's another robot then I'm out," said Cam. "We still haven't worked out what to do with this one."

Megan patted TJ on the shoulder. "TJ knows what he's for, and he'll tell us when he's remembered. Right?"

"And what is Cameron for?"

Megan snorted. "He's mostly here to moan. But he is helpfully tall."

She wandered over to look around the old office space on the right-hand side of the building, while Cam rummaged around an entire wall full of shelves. TJ, eyes alight, peered into the darker areas of the warehouse.

"Y'know Megan, difficult to say whether we've found something when we have no idea what we're looking for," said Cam. "I mean, I've found loads of damp old newspapers and some dead pigeons if that's what we're after."

Megan had wandered over to one of the holes in the floor and was peering down. "Cam, could you come and have a look at this?"

"Not if it means I have to climb down a hole," said Cam, walking over anyway.

"Look." Megan pointed into the hole. "Can you see that?"

The gap opened down onto a dark room, presumably the cellars of the warehouse. But there was something metallic jammed between the stone floor they were standing on and the ceiling beams of the cellar below.

"It looks like a box," said Megan. "Can you reach it if I hold onto you?"

"Think so," said Cam. "It's not too far. TJ, come and anchor us both while I see if I can stretch down."

Cam lay on the floor, leaning into the gap, while Megan sat on his legs and TJ held his feet.

"Got it," said Cam. "It's really light."

It was an old scratched biscuit tin, covered in faded pictures from fairy tales. Megan's hands were shaking as she opened it. Inside was what looked like an old brass coin.

"What is it?" asked Cam. "Is it actual treasure?"

"I'm not sure," said Megan, examining the coin. "It's got strange letters and symbols on it, but no pictures of the Queen or anything."

"Must be really old then," said Cam.

"Do you know what this is TJ?" said Megan.

"I... have seen something like it before. Ago."

"Is it connected to my gran, Sarah?"

There was a crash from outside, dust fell from the ceiling. TJ instinctively moved in front of them.

A creak, then another crash, and they could see bricks falling from the wall in the far corner.

"We'll talk about it later," said Megan, slipping the coin into her pocket. "Let's go."

But Tin Jimmy was heading straight towards the noise and falling bricks.

"Not that way!" hissed Cam.

The brickwork finally gave way, tumbling inwards as a steel wrecking ball pummelled the side of the building, sending pigeons fleeing for the skies.

# CHAPTER 11... SMASH AND GRAB

"You are *kidding*," said Megan "They're knocking it down *right now*?"

A massive black shape was visible through the brick dust, moving slowly forward into the building. At first, they assumed it was a bulldozer, though its odd shape and shadows were confusing. It was Cam who realised first.

"It's Resilience!"

"What?" asked Megan.

"Resilience. You know... the really horrible jaggy sculpture from the roundabout!"

Megan looked, and sure enough, there were the steel beams, now acting as legs; the spheres, now two huge wrecking-ball fists at the end of interlocking steel arms; and the polished silver-and-black glass pyramid, now the dangerous and angry-looking head of...

"A robot!" said Megan. "The sculpture's a robot!"

"Looks like it," said Cam, "and I don't think it likes the look of your robot."

Resilience pounded across the warehouse towards TJ, scattering further dust and debris as he came.

"TJ, get back!" yelled Megan.

Resilience's faceless pyramid head turned towards them, the rest of its body swivelling slowly behind it. It began banging its way towards Megan and Cam instead. Cam seemed to have tuned out completely; he was simply staring in open-mouthed terror. Megan knew there was only one way to escape quickly enough, and it meant doing something really silly. She had been so careful up to now, but the thought of her or Cam being crushed by either the falling building or a giant robot was too much; Megan grabbed Cam and flew straight upwards, darting and weaving like a sparrow through the crumbling roof.

This seemed to wake Cam up.

"Aaaaaaiiiiieeeerrrrgggaaaagghh!" he screamed.

Below, Resilience stopped, tilting its pointed head upwards only once, before rotating back around towards Tin Jimmy.

"You're really heavy for someone so skinny," said Megan. She carefully dropped the stunned Cam behind the fence, some way back from the building. "Back soon. Stay here."

Megan flew back, entering the building through the

hole Resilience had punched in the wall. The damage had already started bringing down huge chunks of the old building. Resilience was currently struggling under some rubble it had brought down upon itself, and TJ was trapped beneath a massive girder that had slipped from the cracked roof.

Megan skirted around Resilience towards him. "You ok?"

"My arms are bending, Megan. The wrong way."

"I'm going to get you out of here," said Megan, glancing around her.

"You are flying," said TJ, "like Sarah."

"Wait, what? Gran could fly too?"

The building rumbled again.

"Tell me later," said Megan.

She pulled and pulled at the girder trapping TJ, and as she did, she saw something moving out of the corner of her eye: a dark grey blur. Resilience had freed itself from the rubble and was crashing towards them, bringing beams and rubble down with it.

"Come on!" Megan hauled at TJ's metal arm, pleading with him to move, but she could not budge him.

Then, something was beside her, pulling at TJ's other arm with the same urgency. She turned to look into the eyes of a huge silverback gorilla. It grinned at her and continued pulling.

Trying very hard not to panic and fly away, despite the kind of day it had turned into, Megan pulled too. Finally the three of them tumbled back down the steel steps of the fire escape and out onto the streets.

The building collapsed further in on itself (like the flan Cam made in home economics last month) then burst into flames (like the flan Cam made in home economics last week).

Resilience was having trouble standing up under the crumbling wreckage, but it was still slowly moving torwards them. Next to Megan, TJ lay crumpled, sparkling and fizzing in a puddle.

"We have to get away!" Megan yelled towards where she'd left Cam – but he was gone.

There was a tremendous thud and a crack, then another. Megan looked back to see that the gorilla had returned to smash Resilience with one of the girders. There was a massive square dent in the side of Resilience's pyramid head as it crashed, at last, to the ground.

Panicking, Megan scanned the area. She knew Cam wouldn't have run off without her. She glanced back at the building, terrified that he might have run back in without her noticing.

Megan turned to TJ, who was still fizzing. "Where's Cam? Did you see him?"

TJ didn't speak, but a low growl from over by Resilience made Megan realise that, in addition to a broken sculpture and a collapsed building, she had another problem to deal with: What do you do with an escaped gorilla?

The big animal was now curled amid the rubble. Maybe it was hurt? Megan was fairly sure that 'Do not approach the gorilla as it may be dangerous' was the usual advice in these situations. So why was she walking towards it?

*I can fly away – straight up if I need to*, she kept thinking to herself.

Curiously, as she drew closer, the great beast seemed to shrink. Its thick black hair receded until there was no gorilla, only the awkwardly crouching body of a boy. He turned to Megan and grinned wonkily.

"You never told me you could fly," Cam said.

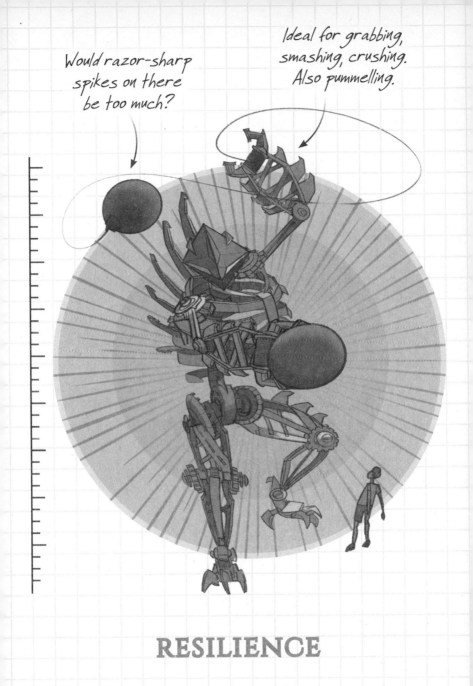

RESILIENCE

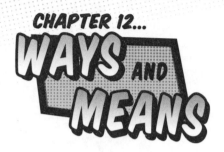

# CHAPTER 12...
# WAYS AND MEANS

Just for a moment, Cam seemed to enjoy having the upper hand. He smiled.

Megan stared, open-mouthed and stunned. And then she punched Cam very hard on the arm. "You were a gorilla!"

"I know," said Cam, rubbing his arm. "I'm not one now though."

"How were you a gorilla?"

"I... can change into animals."

Megan had known Cam since they were three years old. She saw him every single day. How had she not known? "That's... that's really weird Cam."

"So's being able to fly. Or having a pet robot."

"How do you do it?" she asked.

"I'm not actually sure how it works yet," explained Cam. "I can only do a few, and one of those is hamster. How do you fly?"

Megan had trouble explaining this to herself, so she had no idea how to tell someone else. "It's a bit like... the ground and everything else is falling, but I'm standing still. And I just... let it all fall."

"It looked really cool."

"Well, you were an endangered species. Cam this is amazing. I've been keeping this a secret for months. I thought I was going to burst!"

Cam nodded. "I was going to tell my dad, but he's quite allergic to animals. Except snakes. But I can't do snakes."

"I don't know how, but my gran knew," said Megan. "She left me a note with the map. TJ said she could fly too!"

"Your gran could fly? Really?"

"Maybe having superpowers runs in the family?"

"My gran wasn't super," said Cam. "She mostly knitted and drank whisky. Mind you, if she turned into animals it might explain why Dad avoided her so much... maybe he was allergic to her."

Megan hugged Cam happily. Cam patted her on the shoulder, not really sure how best to react. They ran over to TJ, who had stopped sparking by this point, and was gathering himself up.

"We must go. Quickly," he said.

"You're coming to stay with me, TJ," said Megan, as they walked briskly away from the devastation behind them. "And Cam has superpowers too!"

"Yes. I saw," said TJ. "Though I think flying is superior."

For a change, Cam politely ignored TJ.

"How did you find out?" Megan asked Cam, after a thoughtful silence.

Cam knew what she meant. "One morning I woke up and I didn't know where I was. Everything was black, my heart was pounding. I was terrified."

"Oh, Cam," said Megan, "that sounds horrible."

"I eventually saw light and headed towards it, and I fell right out the end of my bed and onto the floor in front of my mirror. It was so strange. I knew I was looking at myself, but it wasn't me in the mirror. It was a hamster. I totally panicked, started screaming, and then all of a sudden I was myself again, shouting at the top of my voice. My mum came running up the stairs; she thought I'd broken something..."

"That's awful," said Megan.

"Wasn't too bad. I did get a day off school out of it," said Cam. "It's happened quite a few times since then, but I'm more in control of it now. I get this sort of fizzing... it starts in my stomach and moves up into my chest," said Cam.

"I get that too! Like fireflies in your tummy."

"That's it, yeah. Been happening for about six months."

Megan frowned. "Seriously, what are the chances of us both having strange powers? Something really weird is going on."

"You're telling me. Secret maps, robots, superpowers.

I wonder if we could get special circumstances at school for all the stress we're under?"

"*Should* we tell someone?" asked Megan. It felt more possible now she was no longer alone.

"Tell them what?" said Cam. "No one's X-raying me and putting me in a freezer. So let's forget telling anyone. It's just us."

"It isn't just us, though, is it?" Megan looked at TJ. "You said my gran could fly too. Do you know what's going on?"

Beneath his blank expression, Megan could tell he was working something out.

"This... has happened before," he said.

"With Sarah?" asked Megan.

"Yes... something... in the water," said TJ. He stared out towards the river, as if hoping that whatever it was would suddenly float to the surface. It didn't.

"That explanation actually hasn't made anything clearer," said Cam. "Do you know why we have superpowers?"

"I can't remember."

"What exactly *can* you remember?" asked Cam angrily.

"Cam!" said Megan. "He's been hidden away for ages; it's all still coming back to him."

"Well, take your time TJ," said Cam. "It's not as if we were just deliberately attacked by a giant robot sculpture."

"Let's hope we finished it off for good," said Megan.

"Yep. Especially because it saw us using our powers."

Megan hadn't thought of that. She didn't mind Cam and TJ knowing she could fly, but Resilience seemed a little less trustworthy. It was the way it had tried to crush her under a building that had really put her off.

"Do you think it was only after TJ?" said Cam. "Maybe it's just like a robot thing."

"It did not seem interested in getting to know me," said TJ. "I seemed to be in its way."

Megan took the coin out of her pocket. "What if it's something to do with this and my gran's map?"

TJ took the coin from Megan, and stared at it once again. "It is possible."

"How would Resilience know about your gran's map?" asked Cam. "Maybe that's just how Waterworx destroys old buildings."

"Wait!" said Megan. "Do you think the other sculptures might be robots too?"

Cam stared at her like somebody who felt that two robots was more than enough to be worrying about right now.

"Remember at the shipyard..." said Megan, "lights and tapping noises were coming from inside Phoenix Egg!"

"And what – you think there was a robot in there waiting to... hatch?"

"It's all got to be connected, don't you think?" said Megan. "The powers, the map, the big robot... we just have to work out how."

"Yeah," said Cam, "piece of bun really."

"We should go to the next place on the map as quickly as we can."

"Oh," said Cam, who had been hoping that getting attacked by a big angry sculpture might have put Megan off exploring for a bit.

Megan smiled. "Me, you and TJ – we just proved we can do anything!"

Cam tried to look inspired and brave, but mostly just managed to look queasy and tired.

# 13. ART AND CRAFT

Mr Finn watched Megan, Cam and TJ struggle through Megan's front door. He had followed them home from the ruined warehouse, and even though he was annoyed about his sculpture getting smashed, it had saved him a lot of bother sorting out building demolition. Every cloud had a silver lining.

Plus, he had always wanted to see the real Tin Jimmy, so that had been nice.

*I wonder if they have any idea what they're getting themselves into,* mused Mr Finn as he turned back to the warehouses to scrape up all the pieces of Resilience. He didn't want any of the parts getting into the wrong hands and ending up on eBay. Again.

At the demolished warehouse, Mr Finn ran his hand over Resilience's battered head. It was going to take quite a bit of hammering back into shape. That wasn't all bad news, though, because Mr Finn actually quite enjoyed hitting things with hammers.

The Waterworx security team were busy hoisting the sculpture onto the back of a truck, while some of the guards were trying to fend off a nosy photographer from the local newspaper.

"Where you wanting this dumped, sir?" said head-of-security Davy. "Scrap yard?"

Mr Finn glared. "Take it to my house, please. I will see to the repairs personally."

"You sure, sir? Because me and the boys reckon you could get a few grand from Big Shug at the yard."

"Thank you for the suggestion," said Mr Finn in a way that made it clear that any further suggestions would result in being sacked, "but this isn't a mashed-up Ford Focus, this is *art*. Big Shug wouldn't know what to do with it."

"Oh, he'd love it. He'd probably just melt it down. He melts most things down."

The rest of the security team backed slowly away from Davy and started looking in other directions.

"Yes. I do enjoy a bit of melting, myself," said Mr Finn. "Of course, I'm more of a dabbler, not a skilled craftsman like Big Shug, art genius."

Too late, Davy realised his mistake. "No sir, I didn't mean… I was trying to be helpful…"

"Being helpful is a pointless waste of time, Davy. Just like you. And to help you remember that in future, you're fired. As of now."

Davy turned to his workmates, hoping for support, but they had all wandered off whistling and looking at their phones.

"Bye Davy," said Mr Finn, waving. "Hurry along now before my terrible sculpture falls on you. You know how easily accidents can happen."

Mr Finn laughed as Davy quickly walked away. The sculpture was carefully loaded onto the truck and driven off into the night.

# CHAPTER 14...
# PAPER AND PENS

TJ had been in Megan's house for two days now, and so far absolutely nothing had exploded or burned down. No one had mentioned that though, just in case they jinxed it.

Rather than jamming him into a cupboard or under a bed, Megan had decided to stick with her story that the robot was a project from school. After all, she did intend to do a bit of reprogramming, so it wasn't a complete lie. This meant that TJ could just stand in her room, plugged in and recharging, in full view of her family. The only tricky bit was making sure no one saw or heard him walking about. So far, so good; her mum had already started hanging Megan's jackets on his outstretched arms. Thankfully TJ was too polite to complain about it.

Cam had rushed over before school because the

Morse-code paper had arrived in the post. He carefully threaded the thin strip of paper into the machine in Tin Jimmy's chest. Despite it only being paper, and TJ being a robot, Cam treated the whole procedure as if it were a delicate medical operation.

"There," he said, rather pleased that he hadn't broken anything or somehow managed to set fire to the paper.

Megan, Cam and TJ all waited, hoping the machine would spring back into life and start printing secret messages. Nothing happened. Cam tapped it repeatedly until TJ asked him to stop.

"Well," said Cam, "it will probably work next time a message comes through."

"There are five."

"We know TJ," said Megan patiently, "and if just one of them sends you a message I'll be happy."

"C'mon, we'll be late," said Cam, tapping the machine once more just in case.

Megan gave TJ a little kiss on the cheek, then she and Cam headed to the bus stop.

"I've been thinking," said Megan.

Cam nodded, looking interested, even though Megan thinking almost always meant trouble.

"Now that we've discovered our powers, don't you think we should be doing something with them?"

"What, solving crimes and stopping bank robberies?" said Cam. "Flying Girl and the Amazing Animal Boy to the rescue!"

"How come you're the Amazing Animal Boy and I'm just Flying Girl?" said Megan. "If I'm anything I'm the Fantastic Flying Girl. Or Fabulous. Yeah, maybe Fabulous."

"Or full of it," said Cam, smiling.

"I feel like we should be helping people," said Megan. "You've read superhero comics. You know how it works."

"Yeah, but those are proper superheroes. I tried turning into a tiger last night and I just ended up with a stripy face and a tail, like a really rubbish Halloween costume."

Megan laughed.

"It wasn't funny. I got stuck like that and had to stay in my room all night. I missed dinner and it was egg and chips."

"Well I keep sleep-flying," said Megan. "I have to make sure my windows are shut every night or I'll probably just float off down the street."

"We're really not that super at all," said Cam, before suddenly brightening. "Do you think costumes would help?"

"You're just looking for an excuse to wear your underpants over your trousers. Again."

Megan was smiling, but Cam knew it wasn't her real smile. "You ok?" he asked.

"It's just... I'm sure the superpowers and the robots are connected to the places on the map," said Megan, "and that's why Gran wanted me to go to them."

"But we didn't find any answers in the last two places we looked."

"Exactly," said Megan, "just more questions. What's the coin for? Why did my gran have a robot? Why were we supposed to find TJ first? Why could Gran fly? Why did the Waterworx sculpture attack us? We don't know anything!"

Over the last few days, Megan had felt angry at her gran for not giving them enough to go on, then bad for feeling angry. Today she was mostly feeling stupid for not understanding whatever it was Gran had trusted her to discover.

"We know loads!" said Cam, putting his hand on her shoulder. "We know your gran has hidden weird stuff in all these old places, we know that at least one of the new Waterworx sculptures is actually a giant murderous robot..."

"And we know where we're supposed to go next," sighed Megan.

"Exactly, we just need to get on with it," said Cam, swiping his phone to bring up their map.

"Number three is Crowfell Hospital," said Megan.

Cam shuddered. "Great, what could go wrong at a creepy abandoned old hospital?"

"Well, it's better than the graveyard, which is where we're going afterwards!"

"You know it must be really bad when that's the best thing you can say about a place," said Cam. "Better than a graveyard."

"So," Megan continued, "can you make it tonight?"

"Not tonight. My mum's backshift starts tomorrow though. You can tell your parents you're at mine and I'll tell Dad I'm at yours."

"Tomorrow then," said Megan, wondering if abandoned hospitals still had old trolleys and bandages in them. "I wonder what we'll find this time?"

"Well, so far we've found a broken robot and a rusty old tin with a coin we can't spend," said Cam. "Your gran was great at stories, but her treasure hunts are rubbish."

Megan suddenly felt a sparkling feeling in her chest – a pulling sensation. Without knowing why, she looked across the road and saw Kirsty McKell's wee brother Jake stepping out onto the street without looking. He couldn't see the oncoming car.

In seconds, Megan had whizzed across the road, pushing him back onto the pavement.

Jake stared at Megan, open-mouthed. The car screeched to a halt and the driver got out of the car to check everyone was ok.

"How did you..." said the startled driver. "You were faster than a..."

Megan reddened. "Thanks, eh... must be the adrenaline. I'd better get to school. Watch where you're walking Jake... Bye!"

Cam waited on the other side of the street, looking just as startled as everyone else. "You do remember about keeping superpowers secret, right?" he whispered.

"I couldn't help it, it was like... a reflex," said Megan. "I was only flying a little bit. The driver just thought I was running ridiculously fast."

"Yeah." Cam smiled. "So fast your feet didn't touch the ground."

Megan grinned back. "I do feel a bit super now. Fabulous Flying Girl to the rescue..."

As if double P.E. in the morning wasn't bad enough, in the afternoon they had more sculpture design. Needless to say, Cam's packed lunch of yoghurt-coated goji berries and whole-wheat breadsticks had not helped him get into the zone.

Kevin had sat beside him all lunchtime trying to talk about their designs. He really was ok when you got talking to him; even better, he was happy to do most of the work on this project. The only problem was that almost every time Cam turned around today, Kevin seemed to be there.

"Maybe we should do a sculpture about all the water power in the area?" beamed Kevin.

"Water power? Sounds a bit Pokémon," said Cam.

"It says here that all the sugar refineries were powered by watermills," said Kevin. "Maybe we should make it a water monster. Did Megan's gran do any books about sea monsters?"

"Hmmm," said Cam. "I think *Serpent Song* was about a sea monster."

"Like a Loch Ness monster kind of thing?" said Kevin, showing Cam a few scribbled sketches.

"Maybe," said Cam, "that one's pretty cool."

Miss McCue had warned them all that today Mr Finn would be coming in to see how their designs were coming along. She had then warned Cam not to mention the freshly smashed sculpture that had been on the front page of the papers.

Despite this, no one was surprised when, as soon as Mr Finn entered the class, Cam stuck up his hand.

"Hello Cameron," said Mr Finn. "Hello Class. How nice to see you again. It's so good to have such enthusiastic pupils."

"Are you going to rebuild Resilience to make it more *resilient*?" said Cam.

Megan stared straight ahead, making a real effort not to glance at Cam, in case that somehow made them look guilty.

Mr Finn took a moment to do the special breathing he had been told to do by the doctor. "Thank you for the suggestion Cameron, but we are talking about *art* here. You don't just repaint a Mona Lisa."

Right now, Megan wished her superpower was telepathy so she could silently shout at Cam to shut up. She decided to jump in before it got any worse. "Are the other sculptures ok?"

"Yes Megan." He nodded. "Evolve and Chronos are both fine." Then he turned to stare straight at her. "I really hope they stay that way."

"Oh, we all do!" said Miss McCue, enjoying this morning's lesson even less than normal. "Vandalism is a terrible thing. We had the police in talking about it last year."

"Quite right too," said Mr Finn. He began wandering around the classroom, slowly picking up their drawings, staring at them and then putting them back down on the desks without saying a word.

"Well," said Miss McCue nervously, "I hope some of our designs will cheer you up. We've had all sorts of ideas. There are sugar molecules, sugar cubes, sugar tongs, a sugar bowl..."

Mr Finn nodded. "All very sweet," he said. Abruptly, he stopped beside Cam and Kevin and picked up Kevin's drawing. "Now, what's this?"

"It's supposed to be, like, a sea monster," said Kevin nervously, "but we were going to make it a bit friendlier."

"That sounds like a good idea," said Miss McCue. "We don't want to be scaring people do we?"

"Oh, I don't know," said Mr Finn, staring pointedly at Cam. "Everyone likes a good scare."

"I'm not sure the school would approve of—" began Miss McCue.

"And what kind of new roof would the school approve of?" interrupted Mr Finn, smiling all the while.

Miss McCue looked unusually flustered and returned to her desk, pretending to look for something.

"I like this, Kevin," said Mr Finn, holding the picture up to the light so he could see it even more clearly. "But I really think it could do with some more teeth, and claws."

Mr Finn put the drawing carefully back down on the desk, and, still smiling, left the classroom without looking at any other designs. Silently, everyone got back to drawing.

"Cam, does he know we broke Resilience?" whispered Megan. "It really seemed like he knew. And your questions didn't exactly help!"

# 15. FACT AND FICTION

<u>The Diary of James Watt</u>      12th December 1811

I can think of nothing but that machine.

By day I work on more plans and sketches for Dalmarnock, but each evening is spent creating this marvelous steam-powered man.

I have taken extreme care to have the parts created in several different foundries so as to keep his construction secret.

He is already capable of several movements. I have come to realise, however, that powering my metal man will be more challenging than I thought. The energy consumption is intensive. However, the basic principles are all in place. He is magnificent.

Mr Finn put down the old faded diary. He had read this page hundreds of times before. Generally, he disliked books; they gave people ideas. Ideas were hard to control. Much better if everyone just got on with the future – watching television or playing their smart phones and tablets like they were supposed to.

He wasn't a big fan of history either: a lot of old rubbish getting in the road of progress. But this project required him to learn about history – the sort of history normal people never got to hear about. Such as ancient robots built by genius inventors.

Mr Finn glanced over at the corner of the room where he had propped Resilience up and battered him back into shape. The sculpture was working again, but there was still a lot of work to do on the electronics.

"My father first got me interested in all this you know," Mr Finn explained to Resilience. "Neither of us liked football and he was rubbish at fishing – too squeamish to pick up worms."

The dented robot's eyes flickered in vague response.

"Oh yes, Professor Finn was quite the robot expert. Always reading these diaries, looking for more information on that blasted Tin Jimmy. He was more interested in the robot than in his own son. Even though I was clearly a genius."

Mr Finn left a short pause here for Resilience to agree with him, before remembering that the sculpture couldn't speak.

"He left when I was thirteen. Never saw him again."

Mr Finn paused again, but this time for dramatic effect.

"That's when I discovered the secret, began to see the truth about the project my father had been working on."

Resilience's eyes glowed briefly once again, as if to say, "Oh really? Please tell me more." At least, that's how Mr Finn chose to interpret it.

He held up some of the pages for Resilience to see. "I'd seen some of his research on James Watt before, but there were more interesting diary entries – secrets father had kept hidden from us."

Mr Finn continued to read, this time aloud to Resilience's unblinking eyes.

It has been many years since I learned the truth about what lies beneath the river, and all that time, I have wondered how best to use my gift to protect what is there. Today, finally, that work is over. The guardians and my robot know what is asked of them. The power beneath the river will be hidden as long as the sigils are kept from falling into the wrong hands.

"Wrong hands!" Mr Finn laughed as he closed the book. "I actually think I have really nice hands," he said, waggling his fingers at Resilience. "Look at those fingernails. Beautifully clean."

He picked up a hammer and wandered over to Resilience to finish tapping out the dents.

"There are still gaps, of course; the notes didn't tell me everything. I know plenty about the Tin Jimmy, and a little bit about the guardians – you and the other sculptures are going to help me deal with those little problems. But it's these sigils…"

Resilience's eyes flickered as Mr Finn began absentmindedly banging him on the head.

"They have to be *somewhere*, hidden away in this *horrible little town*. But what to *do* with them when I *find* them?"

The hammer blows got harder and noisier.

"Father's plans never quite worked out. This time there will be no mistakes. Whatever power is hidden beneath the river… will be mine!"

Mr Finn smashed the remaining dent from Resilience with a resounding clang.

# CHAPTER 16

# DOCTORS AND NURSES

Megan waved to her parents as she wheeled TJ down the drive in the wheelbarrow and set off to meet Cam. It was clear they were quite pleased with all the work she appeared to be doing on this project, which was probably going to make next parents' night even more awkward than usual.

She met Cam at the corner of his road and they set off for Crowfell Hospital, number three on Gran's map. Crowfell was almost two hundred years old, and had previously been a poorhouse, an asylum and a prisoner-of-war camp – so 'abandoned hospital' was actually one of its nicer uses.

As it was out in the middle of a valley, away from the main roads, they wouldn't have to worry about getting caught trespassing. Of course, that also meant that if they were attacked by a killer sculpture, no one would hear them screaming. Well, maybe not – Cam could scream pretty loud, although he insisted on calling it a roar. A really high-pitched roar.

As they approached the fence, Cam looked like he might roar at any second. "So, what treats do you think we'll find in the creepy old abandoned hospital?" he asked.

"Germs. Or zombies," suggested Megan.

"Really? I was hoping for either nothing or a big box of money."

"Are you scared of the hospital, Cam?" asked TJ.

"I'm scared of all hospitals... my mum's a nurse."

Rusted, razor-tipped wire fencing looped all the way around the hospital's grounds. The hospital itself stood dark and empty a little further down the hill and into the valley.

"Looks really jaggy," said Megan, touching the wire.

"I can cut it," said TJ, producing a little blowtorch from the tip of one of his fingers and slicing a hole big enough for them to crouch through.

"Hah!" said Cam. "That's actually the coolest thing I've seen you do so far. You got any other apps?"

TJ's eyes beamed brightly, startling Megan and Cam. He turned and they illuminated the muddy slope that was the only way down towards the hospital. "Full beam," he said.

"I did bring a torch," said Cam.

"Does it have full beam?" asked TJ.

"Well, the batteries are running a bit low..."

"Hmm. Mine is full beam."

The three of them sludged slowly down to the crumbling turrets and boarded-up windows of Crowfell. Its huge wooden front door had been barred with steel beams.

"That will certainly keep most people out," said Megan.

"Or keep things in," suggested Cam.

"TJ, will you be able to move these?" asked Megan.

The robot stepped forward and hauled out the metal bars. The old door creaked open, and TJ's lights revealed a dusty entrance hall and ornate staircase.

"Do you think the lights will still be working?" asked Cam.

"I think we'll be lucky if the floors are still working," said Megan.

"After you, Cameron," said TJ, bowing in a slightly sarcastic way.

"No actually, it's ladies before gentlemen," smiled Megan, even though she didn't really mean it. It just seemed like the easiest way to avoid another argument. She stepped in first and held her breath.

Unlike the tunnels or the warehouse, the silence here seemed still – as if time had broken and stopped. An empty desk blocked their way forward, a dusty old leather chair behind it. TJ and Cam shuffled in behind Megan and they all stood at the desk as if someone was going to sign them in.

"Where should we go first?" asked Cam with unconvincing enthusiasm.

Megan sighed. "I thought it might be obvious when we got here."

TJ had been staring all around the cavernous building, his eye-lights shining into every corner. "I know this place," he said. "I have been here before. Upstairs first."

"Why? What's upstairs?" asked Megan.

"Answers perhaps." TJ stepped onto the stairs, which instantly gave way, leaving both his feet wedged inside the staircase.

Cameron sniggered. "You must be too heavy TJ. Time to switch to unleaded."

Megan flew over gently, stretching her hand out to help TJ up. "Careful TJ, these stairs must be a bit rotten."

The robot stepped out of the hole onto the next step, which he also promptly fell through.

Megan shot Cam a look, but he was already doubled over laughing.

"Tell you what," said Megan, hovering beside TJ, "you grab the banister while I take your arm."

Once Megan and TJ reached the top, Cam began carefully climbing up the banister instead of the stairs.

When he was halfway up, TJ's internal machinery suddenly clicked nervously. Looking all around him, his eyes eventually settled on a stained-glass window at the far end of the corridor. "Did you hear that?" he asked.

"Not funny, TJ," said Cam.

"Shhh!" said TJ. "I am listening."

While TJ and Megan stood still in the dark silence, Cam struggled not to slip off the wonky old banister.

"There. Did you hear it?" asked TJ, this time staring back down the stairs.

"Not a thing," said Megan. "What are we missing?"

Cam scrambled up the banister to where they were standing, trying not to look as if he was in too much of a hurry.

"Whispering children," said TJ. "Can't you hear?"

Megan took Cam's arm. "No TJ, we can't. Are there other people here?"

TJ paused, again staring around the room. "Not any more."

"Ow!" shouted Cam, his arm crushed by Megan's grip.

"I remember..." said TJ, pointing further along the corridor. "That is the room they didn't like."

"Well, let's not go there then," said Cam.

"No, we must go the other way." TJ pointed again and stomped off to his right. He began tearing at the wall, ripping through plaster and wallpaper.

"TJ? Are you ok?" Megan asked quietly.

TJ continued to scrape at the wall. And he exposed a secret door.

Megan and Cam's mouths fell open.

## CHAPTER 17...

# NAMES AND FACES

TJ pushed at the hidden door. "It is locked."

Then, at the same time, Megan and Cam noticed a gap between the door and the floor.

"Could you?" smiled Megan.

Cam shuddered, and then started shrinking. Within seconds, he had disappeared entirely. A hamster scurried under the door gap.

"See," said Megan, "hamster is useful after all."

"Yes," said TJ, "next time I will bring Cameron some peanuts."

There was a rattling on the other side of the door as Cam, now human again, unlocked it from the inside. "It's really stiff," he said. "It must have been locked for ages."

The door creaked open, rust falling from the hinges. The room beyond had no windows, but TJ's lights illuminated it, and they saw that every available space on all four walls had been covered with photos or newspaper clippings. A map of the river was dotted with red pins, and there were many photos of small groups of children standing grimly outside the doors of Crowfell.

"What is this?" asked Cam uneasily. "I'm not liking it here at all."

Megan was peering at all the photos, some of them X-rays.

"There," said TJ, walking towards a rusted filing cabinet in the corner. The bottom drawer squealed as he opened it and reached in, pulling out a green cardboard folder which he handed to Megan.

Slightly confused, Megan opened the folder. It was full of typed-up pages, scribbled notes and right at the back, a list of names, which she read carefully. "My gran's name is on this list," she said quietly. "Why is my gran's name on this list?"

Cam stepped over some broken glass and gently took the list from her. "Do you know any of the other names? John Bone, Tam Ash, Hannah Glass?"

"Don't think so. TJ, do these names mean anything to you?"

TJ looked at the list and blinked. "There are five."

"No TJ, there are only four names here," said Cam, as if he were talking to a troublesome Primary One during a wet playtime.

"Do you know them?" said Megan. "Are they some of the ones who can contact you?"

"John Bone. Here... and in the bomb shelter."

"What did you have to do with this place?" asked Megan, mildly frustrated by TJ's habit of remembering things at a snail's pace.

"Protect."

"What? The children? My gran?" Megan was trying hard not to confuse TJ but the questions just kept coming.

"A secret," said TJ. "Watt's fears."

"Well, you can tell us now," explained Cam, sensing that Megan was about to go off like a firecracker if he didn't start making sense.

"Testing!" said TJ, as if remembering something new. He looked around the room at the photos and X-rays. "All the children here. Were being tested."

"Like in maths and English?" asked Cam hopefully, having finally found a situation in which a maths test was the best option. "Tested for what?"

"Abnormal abilities," said TJ.

Megan and Cam stared at him, shocked into silence.

"My gran and the others," said Megan. "Did they all have superpowers like us?"

TJ nodded. "There are five."

"Ok, that's good TJ," said Megan, "I think. What else do you remember about being here?"

TJ was silent once again, staring around the room. Megan slumped slightly, realising that was probably all they were going to get from him for now.

"I wonder if this John Bone is still around?" said Cam,

trying to rally them both. "Maybe the names were what your gran wanted us to find here?"

"I don't think so," said Megan. "There were actual objects in the last two places."

"Let's have a proper look around then," said Cam. "Seeing some more stuff might jog TJ's memory."

Megan and Cam rifled through dusty drawers and cupboards in the hidden room while TJ stood looking at the faded pictures of children at school, occasionally glancing at the list of names.

"Eh... I think we have a winner," said Cam, crawling out from under a desk, coughing. "This was taped underneath, with scratch marks either side of it."

It was another coin.

"Cam! That's fantastic," said Megan. "Is it the same as the other one?"

"The weird markings on it are different," said Cam, handing it over, "but it's the same size and everything."

"It's coins!" said Megan. "We're supposed to be finding these coins! D'you think we missed one when we found TJ? Or was TJ the only thing we were supposed to fi—"

There was a clatter downstairs

"What was that?" said Cam.

There was another crash, the sound of the stairs giving way again as something tried to get up. Something heavy.

"That doesn't sound good," said Cam.

Together they ran back onto the landing and turned towards the stairs to see another of Waterworx's sculptures – this time the clock-faced statue, Chronos. It was clambering up towards them, ticking and tocking, arms flailing out to grab them.

Without thinking, Megan immediately flew up towards the ceiling, out of reach. "Cam, move!" she shouted, but Cam had already turned into his gorilla form, charging straight towards the robot along with TJ. "No, wait!" said Megan, but it was too late; the combined weight of all three of them completely destroyed what was left of the stairs.

Cam, TJ and Chronos smashed into the floor below in a shower of splinters. Megan swooped down, peering through the thick clouds of dust.

She saw TJ's hand, outstretched, waiting for her. "Megan, quick!" he said. "We have landed on top of the robot."

There was a low growl, which Megan assumed meant that Cam was at least alive. Taking TJ's arm, she hauled him up, one handed, towards the top of the broken stairway.

The dust was beginning to settle, and now Megan could more clearly see a gorilla sitting on the giant legs of Chronos. The robot was struggling, its arms trapped beneath the stairway's broken banister. Its clock hands were whirring angrily around its face.

"Cam, you need to jump up!" shouted Megan. "Hurry, before it gets free. TJ and I will help you."

Cam leaped up towards the broken top edge of the stairs, and gripped it hard, but it crumbled under his weight. Megan knew she would struggle to lift a gorilla, plus she was still holding the coin tightly in her other hand.

Chronos was beginning to get up, scrambling around the banister which had been holding it down. It swiped and grabbed at Cam's dangling feet.

There was only one thing Megan could do. She threw her hands out for gorilla-Cam, but in doing so she dropped the coin. She and TJ each grabbed one of Cam's massive gorilla arms and pulled, dragging him back up to the top floor just as Chronos finally managed to snap the banister in two.

Chronos stopped for a moment, picked up the fallen coin, then continued lumbering up towards them.

"The coin!" said Megan, somehow hoping they'd be able to snatch it back. But Cam was too exhausted to move, panting as he turned back into his human form.

TJ turned to them. "There is no time. Hold on." He lifted them both and ran straight for the stained-glass window. The rotten wood around the old glass gave way easily as TJ smashed through it.

Megan and Cam both screamed as the three of them fell towards the ground.

TJ landed heavily on his feet, aged springs creaking. He let go of Megan and Cam and shouted, "Run!"

The three of them stumbled up the slippery hill back towards the torn hole in the fence. Megan turned only once, to see Chronos staring at them through the broken window, its clock face glowing eerily in the dark.

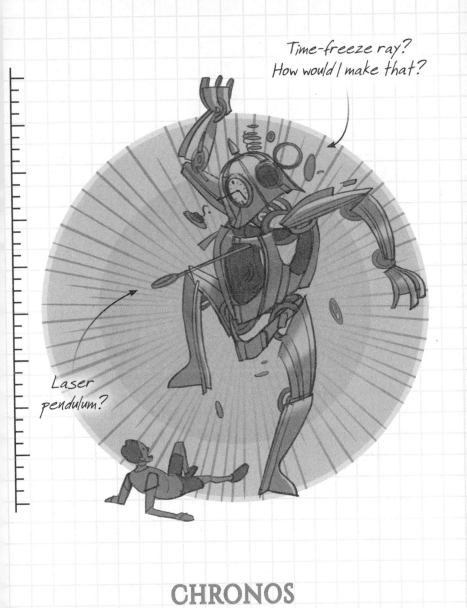

CHRONOS

# 18. OLD AND NEW

Mr Finn's favourite way to relax was to tinker in his lab: unscrew things, hit stuff with hammers, set things on fire… once he even created a death ray while trying to calm down. It fired a relaxing green laser up to two hundred metres.

But there was nothing he could have invented that would calm him down today. He hadn't imagined that the children and the Tin Jimmy would be able to damage his sculptures so badly. He was starting to take it personally, even though the attack had technically been a success.

"Young people today have no respect! And terrible haircuts. They should be locked up! And then fired into space!"

Apart from his collection of discarded robot heads, no one was listening, but Mr Finn was shouting all the same.

"*Months* we've been stuck here," he continued. "Months of searching old offices and abandoned buildings for sigils and any crumpled old bits of paper that might mention Tin Jimmy, the guardians or the river. *And* it's been raining the entire time!"

Mr Finn picked up a robot head and looked it straight in the electronic eye.

"I am getting bored of ransacking old buildings, demolishing them and building shiny new offices in their place to cover our tracks. How can I get to the power under the water when I only have one sigil?"

Years previously, using a few of James Watt's old maps, Mr Finn's dad, Professor Finn, had pinpointed the exact area of the river where the power was supposed to be. At the start of this year, Mr Finn had sent a few of his Waterworx team down there with one of his own inventions, the Seismodulatron, to start exploring the riverbed.

Mr Finn turned the robot head around and pointed to a big box full of cables and bent metal in the corner of the room.

"The Seismodulatron! Nobody else has ever invented anything that can cause miniature earthquakes in small spaces." Mr Finn allowed himself a humble chuckle, then shook the robot head. "But it didn't unlock the power!

The idiots managed to hit an *actual* fault line under the river and create a proper earthquake!"

It hadn't been a big earthquake, but it was big enough for Mr Finn to put the Seismodulatron back in the big box of unused inventions along with the Quantumbler and the Octopants.

"It was after the earthquake that I decided to follow Sarah Stone. She seemed to be the only person still around who was involved last time." Mr Finn nodded the robot head to acknowledge the cleverness of this plan. "I followed her for weeks, hoping I would see something, anything, that suggested she knew about Tin Jimmy or the sigils. But she just did lots of old-lady things like going to the shops on the bus or walking round the dam with her granddaughter. And then she just wandered off on holiday. Useless. I may have lost my temper with her... while holding a hydroboom."

Mr Finn was still sure Sarah Stone had been hiding vital information. He had even forced himself to read all her rubbish books and comics, just in case there were any clues there: *The Moon Pupil, Santa's Little Werewolves, The Boy Who Wasn't There, Candybones*. There were lots of monsters and weird things, but nothing useful like a map or something written in code, which was what he'd been hoping for.

"We need more information," said Mr Finn, putting the robot head neatly on a shelf beside the Defabulator. "The very friendly Mr Garvock from the local museum was telling me about a massive store of James Watt's old pictures and documents that the museum currently doesn't have room to display. Some of the documents were gifted by the noted collector Professor Finn – or 'Dad', as I used to call him."

Mr Finn looked at the shelved robot head once again. "I know what you're thinking... why not ask to borrow it? And I did consider that. But I might need it for a while, so that's why Evolve and I are going to break into the museum and steal it instead. It'll be easier that way. And more fun."

The museum was 150 years old, a friendly looking structure fringed with stone castle battlements.

"Just beautiful," said Mr Finn, gazing up at the expertly crafted turrets and windows, "an excellent site for a new supermarket."

Mr Finn had dressed in his best black tracksuit and balaclava, and brought a sports bag full of gadgets and inventions he thought would be useful during a burglary.

Evolve, standing nearby, was mostly silver, but also a giant round robot, so it was harder for it to blend in.

"Let's be quick," said Mr Finn, "in case someone sees you. Is there a back door I wonder?"

Evolve rolled around to the rear of the building and stopped, flashing its lights at Mr Finn. There, a newer building had been added on to the main structure. It had no doors, but there was a slightly rusty set of metal shutters.

"Right. We could get in quietly that way I'm sure," said Mr Finn.

Before he could work out the best way to do that – perhaps something involving the Magnomatic Beam – Evolve simply rolled forward, smashing through the doors and setting off the alarm.

"What? Why did you…" Mr Finn ran inside the building.

Evolve was waiting beside a pile of stuffed animals he had knocked over.

"Stay here," said Mr Finn, scowling. "Please switch your lights on so we can see, and don't move until I tell you."

Evolve beamed its coloured lights from underneath its circular rim, illuminating rows of old paintings, engine parts and model boats.

Mr Finn scuttled towards some rows of crates at the back of the room, and quickly started reading the contents.

"Dinosaur bits. No. Egyptian treasures. No. Pirate files. No. Watt archive! Three crates?! I knew I should have brought Resilience."

Mr Finn dragged the first crate out. Two smaller ones were stacked behind. "Right. We'll have to hope for the best here. Evolve!"

The robot rumbled forward, its arms unfolding from its huge spherical body.

"Pick these up and run… I mean roll!" said Mr Finn, grabbing the smallest of the three crates.

With the alarm still ringing through the darkness, and the museum's hidden treasures left open for all the world to steal, Mr Finn and Evolve disappeared into the night with boxes full of secrets.

# CHAPTER 19...

# DOTS AND DASHES

Cam had a problem. Usually, Megan would have told him that was because he had a chip on his shoulder, but for once, the problem was not really his fault. Together, they were trying to figure out the best way to solve it on the way home from school.

"So, Mr Finn likes your sculpture design the most for the Waterworx competition," said Megan, "and it turns out there's a fair chance that whatever you make will be turned into a robot."

"Well, if our last two encounters with Waterworx sculptures are anything to go by, then yes – an *evil* robot."

"Correct," said Megan. "An evil robot which may end up trying to smash us and *our* robot."

"*Your* robot," said Cam.

"Whatever," said Megan. "And worse, it looks like it

will probably be a massive scary sea monster from one of my own gran's stories, designed by you and Kevin."

"That about covers it, except the part where Mr Finn requested more claws and teeth," said Cam. "Discuss."

Megan sighed. She had been feeling quite low since she dropped the coin in the hospital. She did drop it while saving Cam's life, and Cam had made a big show of appreciation by buying her a Chinese takeaway on the way home. But she knew it wasn't a good thing that they had lost it.

"Talking of horrible sculptures..." Megan pointed to a lorry that was slowly driving past. Phoenix Egg from the shipyards was securely strapped to its back. A crane truck followed behind, ready to lift it into place in the town square.

"I'm starting to feel a bit outnumbered," said Cam.

"Can't you just convince Kevin to change his design?" said Megan.

"Change it to what?"

"I don't know – something less dangerous," said Megan. "A kitten or something."

"Kittens have claws," said Cam, "and teeth."

"You're right," said Megan, "kittens are terrifying."

They opened the door to Megan's house, and there was an excited stomping as Tin Jimmy battered down the stairs like an oversized puppy. Megan was glad her parents weren't back from work yet.

"Megan! Cameron! The Morse code has worked. I have printed." TJ was brandishing a tiny strip of thin paper with holes in it.

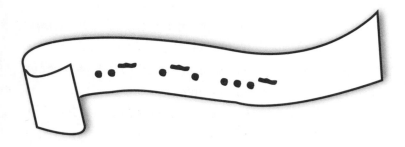

"Seriously?" said Cam, grabbing it from him.

"What does it say?" asked Megan.

"Well, I don't know, do I?" said Cam. "I don't speak Morse. Google it."

Megan was already on her phone doing just that. "Dot dot dash, dot dash dot, dot dot dot dash... urv?"

"Does that help?" asked TJ, sounding almost eager.

"Nope," said Cam, "sounds like we only got part of a word, like 'curve' ... or 'scurvy'."

"Or 'survive'?" said Megan. "Maybe if I hook the Goozberri Five up to the Morse-code machine it'll help download the missing part of the message."

"Well, you do that while I go home for tea. Plus, I've got to work out how to tell Kevin we need to change our deadly sea monster to something cute and fluffy tomorrow."

"Try and think of a nice way to say it, Cam," said Megan. "Try really hard."

"Of course," said Cam, "I'll be extra polite."

Megan hoped that 'extra polite' would take Cam up to the level that most normal people would consider 'basic polite'.

"I'll meet you at lunchtime," said Megan, "you can tell me how it goes."

The beeping started again as soon as Megan took TJ back up into her room. "Is it the rest of the message?" she shouted.

"What." TJ abruptly stood up. "What. What. What."

"TJ, are you ok?"

TJ walked out of Megan's bedroom and stepped towards the stairs. "What. Initiate take off," he said, stepping forwards and not taking off at all. He tumbled noisily down the stairs, landing face-down at the bottom.

Megan ran down after him, relieved again that her parents weren't in to witness it all.

TJ was on the floor, still attempting to walk, like a wind-up toy that had tumbled over. The fall had dislodged the panel at the back of his head. Megan had been wondering about opening it, but not like this...

"Hang on TJ, let me try and help," said Megan, carefully opening the panel and peering inside. A circuit board with a large black microchip was welded to the inside of his head. It had a few different wires connecting to bulbs, other dusty-looking circuits and down towards the Morse-code machine in his chest.

"Well, I'm pretty sure James Watt didn't build this bit," said Megan, carefully pulling at the microchip, loosening it from the circuit board. TJ stopped moving, and the lights in his eyes disappeared.

"TJ? TJ you still there?"

Nothing. Megan pushed the microchip back in. Still nothing.

"Have I broken you?" said Megan, laughing nervously and pretending not to panic. She was feeling bad enough about losing the coin; she really didn't want to have busted her gran's robot as well. "I can't have broken you!"

She thought back to coding club and her conversations with Miss McTeer about what to do when computers didn't work properly.

"You switch them off and back on again." Megan pushed the button on the back of the robot's neck, and his eyes once again flickered into life.

"Megan. What happened?"

Megan stared into the back of TJ's head, deep in thought. "I'm not sure TJ, but I think it's maybe time for some replacement parts. Come on, I've got the stuff in my room."

TJ slowly got to his feet and looked up the stairs. Realising he had fallen, he began checking his arms and legs for breakages. "There have been many replacement parts," he said sadly.

# CHAPTER 20...
# CHIPS AND SAUCE

Everyone in the dinner hall was watching. It was a bit embarrassing.

"No!" shouted Kevin, the angriest Cam had ever seen him. His face was going a bit red.

"I just think..." said Cam.

"You're just jealous because I've done all the work and I'm going to win the Playstation."

"I don't like Playstations," said Cam, "I have an Xbox. And that's not even it."

"What is it then?" said Kevin. "Another one of you and your girlfriend's little secrets?"

"Megan's not my girlfriend," said Cam, who had this conversation with someone at least once a week.

"Then how come you hang about with her more than anyone else?" said Kevin. "The rest of us might as well not be here at all."

"Suits me!" shouted Cam.

"Fine!" Kevin stormed off.

"Well," said Cam, "class this afternoon's going to be really awkward."

Megan walked over with her tray and sat down next to Cam. "Looks like you made a mess of that," she said. "It's no wonder we're outnumbered if we're making enemies wherever we go."

Cam scowled and stole some of her chips.

"Mind you," said Megan, "I've been wondering about that... maybe we aren't as outnumbered as you think."

"How do you mean?" said Cam, taking his secret bottle of tomato sauce out of his schoolbag and squirting it all over Megan's chips.

"If my gran knew other kids with superpowers, and you and I both have superpowers... should we be looking for others?"

"I think we have enough to be getting on with," said Cam.

"But Cam, don't you think other people could maybe help?" said Megan.

"Yeah, only if they're nice," said Cam. "Other people are mostly a pain."

Megan smiled and dipped her chips in the tomato sauce.

"Also, I've had an idea," said Cam. "If I can figure out how to half-transform into things, I could have, like, cheetah legs and totally clean up on sports day this year."

"I think people might notice the spotty legs," said Megan.

"You could do it too," said Cam. "Flying during basketball and long jump?"

"Tempting," said Megan, "I've got double PE next."

The day dragged on in the special way that days with double PE and French do. What made it even worse was how dark it was getting when they finished school, which made the walk home to do homework all the more grim.

On the plus side, it meant that they could sneak around old buildings in the dark without making their parents suspicious. And it meant that it was dark enough for people not to notice unusual things hiding in the shadows. Things like the robot that was hiding in a back street, waiting for Megan and Cam.

TJ couldn't do subtle. He shouted Megan's name and waved.

"TJ! You're supposed to be at home. I left that software installing."

"It has installed."

"Well that's great, but you're not supposed to move about during the day! Someone might see you. Why are you out?"

"We need to go somewhere," said TJ. "Now."

"Why?" said Megan. "Have you blown my house up?"

"No, not yet. My new programming is working. I am remembering," said TJ. "It is the list from the hospital. The names have reminded me of somewhere. A place."

"Somewhere from Gran's map?" asked Megan.

"I bet it's the graveyard," said Cam. "Is it the graveyard?"

"A place not on the map," said TJ. "We must go now. While I remember."

Megan looked at Cam. He looked as tired as she was, but he nodded. They both instinctively turned to their phones to text their usual excuses:

Xtra maths mum. Won't be too l8. xMx

U r a star! Hard work will be worth it!!!

Team practice. Home l8r. Is there pizza

Make sure you shower after. Chickpea soup tonight

"Right, let's go!" said Megan.

"Just let me get a chocolate biscuit first," said Cam, reaching into his schoolbag. "If I'm going to get attacked by another giant robot, I don't want to die hungry. And there's nothing to eat at home anyway."

## CHAPTER 21...
## TRAILS
### AND
## TRACKS

Glancing quickly around to check no one was watching, Cam clambered over the fence and peered down the dark embankment. The remains of an old railway line, now broken and overgrown, disappeared into woodland.

"It's like we're just wandering around looking for the darkest, scariest places in town. And then getting ambushed in them."

Megan shrugged. "Everyone should have a hobby."

"Collecting stamps is a hobby. This is more like a death wish."

Megan and Cam steadied each other as they slipped and skidded down the hill towards the trees. Eventually Megan had to let go of Cam to stop herself from falling over with him.

"Cheers," said Cam, not even attempting to wipe the mud from his trousers.

"Wait for TJ."

The robot was still clambering over the broken play-park fence above the embankment, doing a very awkward job of keeping a low profile.

"TJ, be careful on the hill, it's..."

The robot tripped, skidded and sludged messily down towards the trees. Without a flicker, he stood back up again.

Megan ran over, concerned. "You ok?"

"I am fine. Cameron also fell."

"Yeah, but not quite all the way." Cam grinned.

"It looked like you fell quite far to me," TJ replied.

"Enough!" said Megan. "Is this definitely the place TJ? Can you remember anything yet?"

TJ stared at the old track. Torn cans and old bottles littered the inky darkness. "It is familiar," he said, which was as good as they were going to get.

Together, the three of them started into the woods.

"What is this place anyway?"

"There used to be playing fields round here somewhere," said Cam. "My granda said they used to play football, cricket, all sorts up here when he was wee. Had its own stop on the train and everything. But it just got left and ended up all ruined and overgrown."

"I don't think I'd be playing up here now," said Megan, "even during the day. It feels weird. Creepy."

"Yeah. I remember in primary school Andy McLafferty got dared to run into the middle of the forest. Hardest guy in school. Ran out crying. Brilliant. But I'm starting to think he had a point."

"Are you going to start crying Cameron?" asked TJ.

Megan stifled a giggle.

"Well maybe he saw the Catman," said Cam. "You'd be crying then too."

"Don't start, Cam." Megan kicked an old can, which rattled and echoed around the cutting. "Whoops, didn't mean to do that."

The three of them stood still and silent, waiting for the noise to have woken some sort of monster, because, to be fair, that's the sort of thing that had been happening recently. But the forest stayed quiet, nothing fiendish lunged out of the dark.

"Who is the Catman?" asked TJ.

"I'm not sure I want to tell you," said Cam. "Unless you want to spend the next five minutes being terrified in the dark."

"I do not feel fear. Are you scared, Cameron?"

"The Catman," interrupted Megan, "is supposed to be this old tramp who sleeps in abandoned train tunnels and garages, but some folk think he has a cave up the hills, where he stays with dozens of stray cats."

"That makes him sound nice," said Cam. "You missed out the bit where he kidnaps and eats children."

"No one is totally sure that's true, Cameron," said Megan, rolling her eyes. "I was sure I saw him once, down by the bins in Gran's back garden. She said shipyards round here used to employ a 'cat man', usually just a nice old guy who kept cats to scare the rats away from the warehouses."

Cam jumped in. "Then after the shipyards closed, he went feral, and all his cats followed him, looking for food – and Catman would do anything to keep them well fed. *Anything*." He frowned darkly.

"But no one has seen him for years, Cam. My dad said he used to see him back in the eighties. He'd be ancient now."

TJ clicked and whirred. "Prolonged exposure to the elements reduces life expectancy, especially in a town with so much rain."

"Why is a Catman so hard to believe in?" said Cam. "If I could do cats, I could be Catboy."

"Yes, but you wouldn't live in the dark and eat your classmates," said Megan.

"Dunno," said Cam, "I reckon Big Stevie McGhee would keep you going for a while. He's already sixty per cent hamburger. How far in do you think we are now?"

As they had progressed into the forest, the sky had darkened, there were fewer cans and crisp packets, and the old track had disappeared.

"Keeps his forest tidy at least." Megan smiled.

Cam was checking his phone. "That's me lost my signal. So if he gets us now, I won't be able to call for help."

It was really dark, even with the torchlight and eyebeams, and Cam and Megan realised they hadn't been paying attention to where they were walking. "TJ," said Megan, "I don't think I want to walk on much further. Have you remembered what you're looking for yet?"

"We have missed something," said TJ.

"That's what I was thinking," said Megan.

"Really? I was thinking if we leave now I could still be home in time to watch *River City*," said Cam.

Tin Jimmy stomped forward, further into the dark. Soon they could hear him in the distance, banging and tapping on a rocky mound covered in foliage.

"It is here," he said eventually.

"What is?" asked Megan.

"The secret door."

By the time Megan and Cam had tripped and scuttled out of the trees to where TJ was standing, he had already managed to haul the old door open. It had been disguised with moss and nettles, easy to overlook at a glance, especially in the dark.

Megan peered inside to see light flickering distantly.

"I will go first," suggested TJ.

"Uhm... yep," said Megan, "sounds good."

TJ stepped through into a large cave, with Megan and Cam following a short distance behind. The cave curved around to the left, then sloped downwards. Cam tapped Megan's shoulder and pointed silently at the top of the cave. There were electrical cables running all the way round and down to the light in the distance.

At the far end of the cave, someone had made a little living room, with an old sofa, a gigantic old wooden-framed television set and a bookcase. A ragged and torn curtain hung at the back of this room. TJ stepped towards it to investigate further.

"Ok, *now* do we believe there's someone living up the hills in a cave?" whispered Cam.

Before either TJ or Megan could answer, there was a low growl from behind the curtain.

Nobody had time to react.

The curtain was torn from its hooks as a huge tiger sprung from behind it. Cam and Megan both screamed – Cam just a bit louder. The tiger snarled angrily, displaying impressively massive fangs.

TJ positioned himself directly between the snarling tiger and Megan and Cam.

"Wait, wait, shoosh," whispered Megan, "we're upsetting it."

"Really?" said Cam. "Only I'm quite upset as well."

Cam and Megan began backing towards the mouth of the cave.

The tiger remained ready to pounce, now looking directly at TJ. It wasn't calming down even though they were retreating.

And then it pounced, knocking TJ over and pinning Cam to the cave wall with its massive paws.

# CHAPTER 22...
## TIME AND AGAIN

Megan took off and launched straight towards the tiger. Cam had instinctively turned gorilla, and was now, along with the tiger, taking up almost half the space in this tiny makeshift room. He pushed out, forcing the tiger back, while TJ scrambled to his feet and together with Megan, hauled the beast away from Cam.

It took them both a moment to realise the big cat wasn't fighting back. The tiger looked from TJ to Megan to Cam. Gorilla-Cam raised his fists, preparing to end the argument, and knocked over the TV.

The tiger growled once more, then began to change, its teeth and fur retracting until only a straggle-haired, scrawny old man remained. He stood up slowly, steadying himself against the bookcase, sweeping his grey hair from his eyes. Seeing this, Cam also transformed back to his human form, staring at the old man all the while.

The old man stepped towards TJ first.

Megan stepped protectively in between them, holding a hand out as if to keep him away. "Stop right there!"

"Careful Megan, he's stronger than he looks," said Cam, still shaking slightly from the transformation.

"Sorry... you surprised me," said the old man, shaking his head. "Really sorry... are you all ok?"

"No, a tiger just attacked me!" shouted Cam, checking himself for tiger cuts.

"Yeah... and then a gorilla knocked over my telly."

"Who are you?" said Megan.

The old man looked at the robot and shuffled awkwardly.

Cam glared at him as he dusted himself down. "Megan, I think this is the Catman."

The dishevelled man shot Cam an angry glance. "Don't call me that."

"Come on! Giant cat that roams the hills, strange old man that lives in a cave." Cam pointed. "Catman."

"But I don't eat children," said the Catman. "Though I'm considering making exceptions."

TJ had not spoken or moved since the tiger had transformed. He just stared at the Catman, clicking and whirring in thought.

"You left me," said TJ at last. "You tied me up in the bomb shelter and left me."

The Catman hung his head.

"*You* did that?" said Megan.

"There was no light. Only the damp air, and my body slowly rusting. Thoughts disappearing," said TJ. "You told me to wait. I did not know how long for."

Megan took the robot's hand.

"I was trying to keep him safe," protested the Catman. "Is TJ still here? Yes. Did they find him? No. See? Safe."

"Did *who* find him?" asked Megan, suddenly delighted they'd found someone else who might be able to give them some answers.

The Catman looked at her, and back to TJ, "Is that... is she..."

"Megan Stone. Granddaughter of Sarah Stone."

He stared at her for a moment, before quietly saying, "You are so like her."

"You knew my gran?" said Megan uneasily.

He nodded sadly. "A long time ago. I'm really sorry for your loss. And I was a big fan." The Catman pointed to his bookshelf, where there were rows of Sarah Stone books – even lots of copies of the same ones, but with different covers.

Cam had started quietly picking up the bits of smashed television screen. "I'm sorry I turned into a gorilla and smashed up your living room," he said.

"It happens more often than you'd think." The Catman grinned. "Though normally it's a grumpy tiger or a lonely polar bear doing all the damage. How did you find me?"

"Sarah Stone left Megan a map," said TJ. "We followed it to Crowfell hospital and I remembered you. John Bone."

"Wait. John Bone from the hospital list is the *Catman*?" said Cam.

"Please stop calling me that," sighed John. "And Jimmy, what d'you mean you remembered me? Impossible to forget what we all went through."

Megan stepped forward. "TJ had no memory when we found him. I've been updating his software."

John winced. "So he hasn't filled you in? Sarah didn't plan for that?"

"Filled us in on *what*?" Megan asked.

"It's starting again," said John Bone. "I thought so. I've got a lot to tell you."

CHAPTER 23...
HEART
AND SOUL

John, still in his cave living room, was jogging on the spot and stretching, as if preparing to run a race. "Sounds like it's time to finish the job we were all born for." He turned to TJ. "Do you remember anything about the last time we were all together?"

"Pieces. Not everything," said TJ.

"What are you talking about?" said Megan. "When were you last all together? What job?"

John was practically dancing around his cave now, clearly very excited. "Your job, Megan, and your gran's before you," said John. "And gorilla-boy's, and mine, and Jimmy's. We're guardians."

"Guardians of what?" asked Cam, still hoping that this treasure hunt might actually feature some treasure.

"The sigils!" said John. "I take it you've got the sigils?"

"What are sigils?" said Megan.

John looked at TJ. "Have you forgotten that too?"

"There are five," said TJ.

"That's right Jimmy," said John. "Five sigils, one for each guardian. Sarah had to hide them, remember?"

"The coins," said Megan, "are the sigils like coins?"

"Yes!" said John. "Do you have them?"

"My gran left me a map... we haven't found them all yet," said Megan. Cam shot her a warning glance. "So my gran was one of these... coin guardians?" asked Megan, changing the subject.

"It wasn't the coins themselves we were guarding, it was what they could *do*," said John.

"So what can they do? Why did Gran hide them?" asked Megan.

John ignored her, walked over to his bookshelf and pulled one of Sarah Stone's books out slowly. "Your gran... was magnificent. She dipped and twirled like a beautiful bird on the wind."

John handed the book to Megan. Inside was an old photo, yellowed and creased, of her gran as a young girl. She knew this not because she had seen lots of pictures of her gran when she was young, but because it was like looking in a mirror. Standing beside her was a handsome boy with a lopsided grin and scruffy hair.

"I had better teeth then." John smiled, rather proving his point. "So how long have you been flying?"

Just for a moment, Megan was caught offguard by the

question; it was asked in such a matter-of-fact way, as if it was no longer a secret.

"A few months," she said. "I'm still learning."

"Course you are," said John. "The smartest folks are always learning."

John then stared carefully at Cam. "I know your powers best of all. What can you do? Wolf? Eagle?"

"Hamster," said TJ.

"And gorilla! I can do gorilla, you saw me!" protested Cam.

"So," said John, "has it been easy finding the sigils?"

"Really easy apart from the giant robots," said Cam.

"Giant robots?"

"Yeah, they've turned up at two of the places on the map so far," said Megan, wondering when it had become normal to talk about giant robots.

"And have these robots attacked you?" asked John, sounding genuinely concerned.

"Well... pretty much," said Megan, "but they haven't managed to hurt us badly yet."

"I smashed one of them right up," said Cam, who was really happy to be able to tell someone else about that.

"Gorilla?" asked John.

Cam smiled and nodded.

"How many sigils have you got now?"

"We found two," said Megan, "but we lost one. Should we have found one in the tunnel where TJ was hidden?"

"I don't know. Only Sarah knew where the sigils were

hidden. But I doubt she would have hidden TJ's sigil where we planned to hide TJ himself."

"Why did only Sarah know where they were?" asked Cam.

"We were all in charge of one sigil each at first – our own secret, passed down through our families – but when we got into trouble Sarah protected us all by hiding them herself." John looked away at this point, his shoulders low and heavy. "Those robots will be wanting the sigils just like Clutha Chemicals did back in the day, Jimmy."

If TJ recognised the name, he did not respond.

"Who are Clutha Chemicals?" asked Megan

"Really nasty bunch," said John. "They were the ones doing all the tests at Crowfell Hospital."

For some reason, the name seemed familiar to Megan, but she couldn't think why. Perhaps she'd heard it in one of her gran's stories.

"I can tell you all about that later," said John, "but if these robots are after the sigils, whoever programmed them is up to no good. We need to be ready for them. I can help you."

John smiled wonkily and put his hand out for them to shake.

Megan wasn't convinced. "I want to believe you. But if my gran knew you were here all this time why did she never mention you? Why did you never visit?"

"I did!" said John. "Now and again. Your gran and I

would meet in secret. But it wasn't safe. They might still have been watching..."

"Who might have been watching?" Cam asked loudly.

"And you still haven't told us what the sigils are for! How can we be guardians if we don't know what we're guarding?" asked Megan, annoyed at herself for getting distracted by John's photograph and his questions about flying. "You haven't given us any proof that we should trust you. It's not like Gran put this place on the map."

John ran his fingers through his long, lank hair, and shook his head. "I can explain everything," he said, "but not all at once, not right now." John looked like he was in pain, and faint stripes rippled across his face before disappearing.

"Why not?" said Cam. "Why should we believe you? You could be anyone."

"You attacked us when we came in!" said Megan.

John leaned over and made a low noise. To Megan it sounded eerily like a growl – not an angry growl, but the sound of a trapped animal.

TJ stepped in front of the Catman. "He is John Bone. There are five. Stone is one. So is Bone. You can trust him."

Cam glanced at John, whose face was still rippling with stripes, then back at Megan. He gave a nod only she would have noticed. She knew he meant they'd learned all they could today and should head home. Carefully, still slightly unsure, both of them shook John's hand.

"Thank you," said John, "thank you."

He took one of TJ's hands as well, then slapped him on the shoulder. "Jimmy, where you staying right now? There's always room for you here."

Megan and Cam stared around the tiny cramped room, not entirely convinced, but it was becoming more and more difficult for TJ to stay hidden at home. Maybe it wouldn't be such a bad idea.

"Just one thing I'm not sure about," said John. "Where are the others?"

"What do you mean?" said Cam. "There's just the three of us."

"No other friends?"

"We're hanging about up the hills at night with a rusty robot and a tramp," said Cam.

"We don't really do parties," explained Megan.

"No. I mean, there should be more guardians, more of you with powers," said John.

"There are five," said TJ.

"We did wonder... TJ says that a lot," said Megan, "but we didn't know how to find out."

"Is there, like, a special guardian signal or a secret base or anything?" asked Cam, looking round and hoping this wasn't it.

"Afraid not, Cam," said John. "We're going to have to figure things out on our own again."

In that moment, Megan saw something flicker across his face, the same troubled look she'd watched her gran fail to hide that day at the dam. "Did you all figure things out ok last time?" she asked.

John smiled sadly to himself, as if he were reacquainting himself with an old memory. "Enough stories for tonight, eh? You'd best get home. Need your rest."

"How come?" asked Cam.

"Because tomorrow, you begin training to be superheroes."

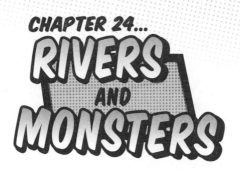

# CHAPTER 24...
# RIVERS
# AND
# MONSTERS

It was one of those rare, glorious autumnal Sundays which turn up after three or four weeks of grey rain. On those blue-sky days, you could see the mountains across the river stretching off towards the Highlands. The river itself was still as glass, reflecting the two medieval castles that stood on opposite shores. Even the gap sites and rubble at the riverside looked pleasant.

So a morning walk up into the moorland behind the town wasn't a bad idea. Going on that walk with a shape-changing old man and a badly rusting robot maybe wasn't so clever.

Megan and Cam had spoken for hours about whether they should trust John Bone or not – mostly they were taking TJ's word for it. But then again, TJ still couldn't remember everything yet. The only thing they were both sure of was that John had tied TJ up in the bomb shelter. Cam insisted he could totally sympathise with this, but all the same, it seemed a bit much. Eventually they had decided that if John turned out to be evil, Cam would turn into a hamster and bite him, then Megan would fly them both away. It wasn't the best plan, but it was all they had right now.

"I don't think I realised there was this much countryside behind the town," said Megan, staring around wide-eyed.

TJ had stomped ahead towards the brow of the next hill to survey the area. "This will do," he shouted, shattering the silence and startling birds. "Low visibility from roads, no overhead cables."

John waved his approval. "Right you two, run up there and..."

"Sorry what?" said Cam. "Run?"

"Yes run," said John. "We're here to train. You need to be fit to fight giant robots."

"Is this going to be like extra PE?" asked Megan. "Because if it is, Cam will get a note from his mum."

Cam scowled at Megan. "Very funny."

"Seriously. Only it usually says 'Please do not excuse Cam from PE – he needs the exercise'."

"My mum's a nurse," explained Cam.

"Very good advice," said John. "Now, go! Don't make me turn into a tiger."

For a moment, Megan and Cam stood still, assuming he was joking. Slowly, yellow and black stripes started spreading across John's face, his toothy grin sharpened.

"Go!" yelled Megan.

Up on the hill, the moorland plateaued out, stretching for miles of flat, empty green and brown. Cam puffed up the slope behind Megan. "Blimey, that's a really boring view."

"No it's not. It's beautiful."

"Needs more cows," said Cam.

John arrived shortly after them. "Y'know if I'd been you two, I'd have flown up, or turned into a rabbit or something to get up here sharpish."

"You said run," said Megan.

"D'you always do what you're told?"

They looked at him blankly.

"Right. From what I've just seen we've got a lot of work to do, and not much time. I'll be expecting you both to be out exercising as often as possible, whether that's flying or galloping or whatever. Up here you can practise your powers without being spotted. Ready for your next task?"

Megan and Cam nodded, though mostly out of fear and politeness.

"Megan first. I want you to fly, just from one end of this field to the other."

Megan immediately began floating up towards the blue sky.

"...Ah no. I mean really low. So close you can touch the moss."

"Won't I bump into things?"

"Only if you're not careful." John smiled. "Now, Jimmy will keep an eye on you while I put Cam through his paces."

Cam groaned. "This is actually going to be worse than PE."

For the next hour, Megan dodged and weaved between stray rocks and heather, while John had Cam change quickly between rabbit, gorilla and even hamster.

"The change itself takes a lot of energy, so you're always going to feel a little weak when you've first turned."

Cam, now simply Cam again, crouching and out of breath, nodded. "Totally," he gasped.

"But you can't let them know that. So for those crucial few seconds after you change, use whatever you have that allows you to keep still. Distract them with a roar, rear up as if you are about to bite. Hiss and squawk. Whatever. Half the time they'll run, giving you a wee chance to get yourself together."

Cam took a swig of his bottled water.

"Your main problem will be low blood sugar and dehydration. Animals burn calories faster than we do, so be sure to drink plenty of sugary drinks."

"Wait," said Megan, looping slowly over the field, "isn't that really bad for him?"

"Shut up, Megan, this is the best advice I've been given since this all started."

"Yeah, but not for your teeth," said Megan. "He has nice teeth John, don't let him melt them."

"I think you should drink the sugary juice," said TJ.

Cam frowned at him.

"How are you getting on?" John asked Megan.

"Well, I'm managing ok on low flying but..."

"Right. Good. Now do the same thing again, but on your back."

"Eh? How will I see?" asked Megan.

"You ever swim on your back?"

"Yes. But..."

"Like that, but without water," said John, miming a backstroke.

"Make Cam do something hard as well," said Megan.

"That's the plan," said John, grinning over at Cam. "You can only change into a few things just now, right?"

"Yes. I'm still not totally sure how."

"It's to do with how well you can visualise particular animals. Let me guess... there's a gorilla poster in your room, and you've had rabbits and hamsters as pets?"

"No gorilla poster," said Cam, "but I do play 'Donkey Kong' quite a lot."

"Right. So, you just need to get to know more animals in the same way. Useful animals."

"Can you show me how to be a werewolf?" asked Cam. "No! Lion! No! Yeti!"

"Yetis aren't real!" laughed Megan as she lay on her back just above the grasstips.

143

"Incorrect," said TJ. "I once encountered them in caves beneath the Kremlin."

"TJ apparently had all these other adventures before we met him," said John. "We were never quite sure how much to believe."

"Neither are we!" laughed Megan.

"Believe in yeti," said TJ. "They bite."

"What is it like being a guardian? What do you do?" asked Megan. "I just can't imagine my gran keeping quiet about it and staying out of trouble."

"No, she didn't," said John. "None of us did. Same with you two. You should run *towards* trouble, because chances are, it will be trouble you can fix."

"We haven't fixed much so far," said Cam. "Mostly some buildings have fallen down."

"Trouble will find you anyway," said John, tapping his chest. "You'll feel it, right here. Pulling at you."

"Yes!" said Megan. "We get that, the fireflies flickering at your chest."

"That's how you know," said John. "When you feel like that, there's trouble nearby. You'll be drawn to it."

TJ was staring silently at the river again.

"Enjoying the view, Jimmy?"

"The river. We watched the river. Protected it."

"That's it Jimmy, it's coming back to you."

"What was in the river?" asked Megan. "Is that what the sigils are for?"

John nodded grimly. "More or less. There's something

down there, something old. People who become guardians, like me and Sarah and the rest of us, are supposed to stop it getting into the wrong hands. But from my generation there's only me left, and I'm retired. So it's your turn to do the same."

"It's never my turn," said Cam. "I'm last in the queue, last pick at teams and that's the way I like it. Now, let's go yeti!" Cam looked to Megan for a laugh, but she seemed to be deep in thought.

"Listen," said John, "let's start simple and save the monsters for another day. You've only just mastered hamster."

John's skin gradually turned green and scaly, very slowly, so that Cam could watch how to become a lizard.

"Ugh, I hate lizards," said Megan, flying higher up.

Lizard-John nodded to Cam as if to say, *Now you.*

Cam began going green, laughing as a forked tongue popped out from between his teeth.

"Rivers and monsters," Megan whispered to herself. "Rivers and monsters." Those words hung there, before drifting gently away like the dandelion seeds she'd been swishing past all afternoon. *I've forgotten something,* she thought, *something important.*

## 25. HIDE AND SEEK

In his lab, Mr Finn put down the blowtorch and stared again at the pile of his father's notes and diaries in the corner. He was trying really hard not to just set them on fire.

"No. I don't get it. It makes no sense." He turned to look at spiky Resilience and clock-faced Chronos, who were both in the lab tonight receiving some new weaponry. "Does it make sense to either of you?"

Neither of the robots could talk, shrug, or even shake their heads, but Resilience flashed his eyes in response.

"Why was the Tin Jimmy so important to Dad's plans?"

Chronos swivelled slightly to look at Resilience, hoping the thornier robot would have a better idea of what to do in this situation.

"I mean the so-called 'master control signal' doesn't

even work! And the tracking device isn't much better. Runs slow half the time. Total amateur!"

Resilience flashed his evil red eyes sympathetically.

"Its systems have probably rusted away to nothing wherever it was hiding for fifty years," said Mr Finn, shaking his head. "Shoddy workmanship."

Mr Finn was now talking directly to the big pile of books. "*This* is how you build robots," he said, gesturing to Chronos and Resilience. "These robots do what they're told."

Resilience and Chronos both flashed their eyes in appreciation. Mr Finn was actually being a bit generous here because, to be honest, so far Resilience had been flattened by a building and Chronos had been half-destroyed by a collapsing staircase. Not to mention Evolve who had recently bungled the burglary at the museum.

Mr Finn was so busy being angry and creative that he didn't hear the regular beeping of the tracking signal. Chronos had to ring its alarm-clock head to stop him drilling holes in things.

"What? What is it I'm... oh. I wonder if they're out searching again." Mr Finn brought the map up on his computer screen. "He's up in the hills. Why is he up in the hills? Robots don't need fresh air and exercise. Odd. Still, worth checking out just in case."

He searched around for the device he used to communicate with each of the sculptures, pressed a button and cleared his throat. "Evolve?"

147

Far off, near the dam where it was positioned as a public work of art, the spherical robot rolled upright, standing as near to attention as it could.

"Fetch," said Mr Finn.

# CHAPTER 26...
# SPRINGS
## AND
# MAGNETS

It was breakfast time on Monday before Megan realised what she had been missing, as if, like TJ, the cogs and wheels in her head had been quietly working away on the problem overnight.

"The old newspaper!" she shouted at her mum, who spilled her Shreddies in surprise.

Megan thundered upstairs to her room and took her gran's letter out from the little china-print box, carefully unfolding the old scrap of newsprint. It was dated September 1964. There were several stories, but only now did she realise they were connected – the photo was of Crowfell hospital, and the main story...

# GAZETTE

Thursday, September 17, 1964

# MYSTERY FISH WASHES UP AT BEAUTY SPOT

Local sunbathers in Gourock were in for a shock yesterday when an unidentified creature was found on the shore. Measuring more than 12 foot long, it was initially believed to be a large eel. The area was quickly closed off to ensure safety from potential toxins, and scientists from local firm Clutha Chemicals were on site to carefully remove the mysterious carcass.

It is not the first time Gourock folks have thought they had their own Loch Ness Monster: during the Second World War another strange creature was washed up at Cardwell Bay. Following investigation, this particular sea monster – believed to be a basking shark – was buried beneath the football pitch of a local primary school.

# LOCAL TEAM

Next to the article, there was a photo of some serious-looking men in white coats standing by the riverside, pointing. John Bone had told them it was Clutha Chemicals doing experiments on children at Crowfell Hospital.

*These things must be related*, Megan thought.

Before she could wonder much more about it, she heard the special frantic banging at the door that meant Cam had arrived.

"I'll get it Mum!" said Megan, because the less time Cam spent trying to sound polite in front of Megan's mum, the better.

"Well, there's good news and bad news," said Cam. "The good news is, we actually don't have school today, school's shut. A bit of the roof caved in again."

"Really? Brilliant, we can train!"

"The bad news," said Cam, "is that last night, John saw Evolve rolling around the hills. He went all cheetah and sprinted over to tell me this morning. He thinks it might have been looking for TJ."

"How did it know we were there?"

"That's what worries me," said Cam. "The cave's well hidden by the trees and the valley, so I don't know how it could have known we were there..."

"Maybe we should go and check out Evolve," said Megan.

A quick search of Evolve and the surrounding area didn't reveal anything useful. Cam had even taken the opportunity to turn into a beetle and scuttle in and out of the sculpture's nooks and crannies just to be sure. But tiny scuffmarks of grass and mud suggested John had been right about Evolve rolling round the hills after them.

So now they were sitting on a bench across the street, waiting to see if the statue did anything unusual. While they sat, Megan quietly explained what she had found in the old newspaper clipping.

"Burying monsters under school football pitches? Seriously? Surely that's just asking for ghosts," said Cam. "How long has this stuff been happening?"

"Probably for much longer than we think," said Megan.

"Do you think that's why the science department smells so bad?" wondered Cam. "Because there's a dead sea monster under it?"

"No," said Megan, "it smells bad because none of the science teachers use deodorant. Also, sulphur."

"We should dig this creature up!" said Cam.

"It's hardly going to be there now, is it? It was buried fifty years ago."

"So was your robot," said Cam.

You could just about see the river from this part of town. Megan had found herself staring out towards it much more since their conversation with John Bone.

Calming curves
and circles.

False sense
of security.

**EVOLVE**

Cam saw her looking. "Do you think that's what they were protecting then? A monster?"

"But the monster died, so why would they still be hang—" Cam stopped, grabbed Megan's arm and pointed to the statue. "It moved. I'm sure I just saw Evolve move."

Megan peered over at it. "Well it's not moving now."

Although Evolve was a spherical sculpture, it stood near the dam in what someone had decided to call a 'sculpture garden', which was all sharp angles and pyramid shapes. Naturally this meant people were always using it as a playground or a skate park, and hardly ever as a sculpture garden, whatever that actually was.

"A real skate park would probably have been cheaper," said Cam, as another BMX smacked up against Evolve. "So are we staying here all day?"

"Well, I could get TJ to hack into the CCTV, instead."

"How does that work? Surely he's... not very digital."

"He's now almost fully Goozberri-Five-powered, off a solar plate in his head."

"Ha! He's getting even more like one of those Lego robots," laughed Cam.

"At least I'm not actually helping build another robot sculpture to attack us!"

Cam shuffled uncomfortably. "Yeah, well."

The conversation stopped abruptly. They both stared at one another.

"Did you feel that too?" asked Megan.

"That fizzing?" said Cam, tapping his chest. "Yeah."

"No... more than fizzing this time – more like... magnets, pulling..."

The two of them stood up suddenly.

"We run towards trouble, right?" said Cam.

It was slightly easier for Cam to use his powers in broad daylight than it was for Megan, providing he didn't turn into anything too exotic. Having assumed that the park would already be full of squirrels, he was off and running. Megan picked up their backpacks and ran after him, wondering whether people wouldn't realise she was flying if she hovered very low.

The dam was slightly pretty and quite dangerous, like Sandra McKee in their class. It invited dangerous ice walks in winter, and dangerous nesting swans that hissed and flapped in spring and summer. It was also an excellent spot to sail model boats. There was even a specially built jetty jutting out from the muddy shore.

Cam immediately spotted the problem. There were small splashes and bubbles just a few metres from the jetty's edge – someone had fallen in. Only half sure of what he was going to change into, Cam dived into the murky water.

To stay unnoticed, Megan half-ran, half-flew closely behind. She arrived at the water's edge just as Cam disappeared. "Cam! No!"

Cam was usually a rubbish swimmer. Even with armbands on he flailed like a broken octopus. But today he was sleek, swift and determined.

He could see the boy, struggling, caught in the reeds.

Cam tore and chewed his way through the tangled plants, trying to free him. The current was against them, pulling them both further down, but Cam nudged the boy urgently.

Panicking, the boy understood enough to know what he had to do. He pushed himself upwards, arms flailing, trying to grab at anything. And then something grabbed him. Megan flew low, dragging the boy quickly onto the jetty. He coughed and spluttered, blinking in the sun.

"Are you ok?" asked Megan, reflecting how little first aid she remembered from that one time she went to Guides.

The boy nodded, still coughing.

"What's your name?" she asked.

"Richard," he spluttered. "I'm Richard. I slipped and then... How did you...?"

Back in human form, Cam pushed himself up onto the jetty. "I think we should get you home, Richard," he said. "Sounds like you might be in shock or something."

"An otter rescued me," said Richard.

"Of course it did, Richard," said Megan. "Come on, let's go."

As they walked Richard through the small crowd of BMXers that had gathered around, Megan couldn't stop smiling. She knew you were probably supposed to look all serious after rescuing someone, but actually, she was totally delighted. She stole a look at Cam, who was also grinning from ear to ear.

At the other end of the dam, just out of sight, a girl stood watching them lead Richard away. She bit her nails nervously the whole time. When the drowning boy and his rescuers were out of sight, she began absent-mindedly twirling her fingers through the air in front of her, and as she did, tiny waves and whirlpools appeared in the nearby water, then gradually calmed.

## CHAPTER 27...

### GODS AND MONSTERS

Even though they were up the hills behind the town in a cave hidden by forest, there was still a fair chance that people could have heard Megan shouting.

"John, it was amazing! We totally saved someone's life!"

"I think that should count as today's training session," said Cam, rifling through John's cupboards, hoping for chocolate digestives.

"We have run out of biscuits," said TJ, handing Cam a stale-looking pink wafer.

"How did you both do it without being seen?" asked John. He looked as pleased and excited as they were.

"I sort of hovered," said Megan, "flying really close to the ground like you showed me!"

"Brilliant," said John, beaming with pride, "and what did you change into?"

"Otter," said Cam, spitting wafer crumbs everywhere. "It's basically just a soggy hamster."

"This is great," said John, "two real-life superheroes!"

TJ brought Megan a cup of tea and some chocolate digestives. Cam frowned at his pink wafer.

"John," said Megan, "see what you were saying about something in the river? I remembered my gran left me this old clipping." Megan handed the newspaper to John. "Was this what you meant?"

"Not the fish or the eels," said John, reading the page, "but this was the start of it all for us."

"What's in the river, John?" she asked. "Why is it so important?"

"Ok," said John, sitting down in his torn chair, "I'll tell it to you as it was told to me. Almost three hundred years ago, not long after the very start of our little town, there was a storm. Strange lights filled the sky and a great meteorite crashed to earth, right into the Clyde. A few of the folk who had seen it from the shore rowed out to where it had sunk, and a green glow surrounded their little boat, bubbling and boiling. They were terrified. The wind stirred up again and their boat capsized, dropping them into the green, broiling depths."

"Did they drown?" asked Megan.

"No, they didn't," said John. "Somehow, much later, all five of them found their way safely back to shore. Though they were alive, they were changed."

"They got superpowers?"

"You could call it that," said John. "Back then people displaying superpowers would have been accused of witchcraft and burned at the stake. Nowadays people would probably explain it as genetic mutation caused by whatever element fell to earth in that meteorite – hence all the freaky mutated fish monsters that kept washing up on the shore. Either way, those who had been in the green glowing water knew they had to protect the source of their powers from being discovered and misused by others. They became the first guardians, and their gifts and responsibilities were passed down through their family lines."

"So where do the sigils fit in?" asked Megan.

"Well, the son of one of the first folk out on the wee fishing boat was James Watt, the famous inventor."

"The James Watt that made TJ?" asked Cam.

"The very same," said John. "He inherited his father's super-intelligence, and he began to realise he had a talent for invention and engineering. He also understood that unless they guarded that power under the water, it could be used for terrible things. He took a diving bell out onto the river, and plunged down to try and discover the truth about what had fallen from the sky that night, and what he could do to protect it."

"What did he find?" asked Cam.

"He never revealed it," said John. "But whatever it was, Watt decided to build an unbreakable shield around it. It took him years: his life's work, his most amazing invention, carried out in secret. And to make sure his shield could only be opened by the guardians, he created a locking mechanism for it; one that needed five keys."

"The sigils?" said Megan. "Are the sigils the keys?"

"That's right. One was given to each guardian, and passed down through their family. Only all five together would ever be able to unlock the shield. Finally, Watt built a guardian to take his and his children's place," said John.

"Why?" asked Cam.

"Because people had started to talk in the town. He knew someday his family might be in danger, and while super-intelligence was one of the easier powers to hide, it doesn't make you very strong in a fight. He wanted his descendants to live lives as normal as possible. So he poured his knowledge into a machine that he hoped would stand guard for centuries in his family's place. A machine that had to be kept secret because it was so advanced."

Megan and Cam looked over at TJ. Because he was a bit forgetful and clumsy, it was easy to forget just how amazing he actually was. Like he had always said, he was built to protect.

"Does that mean Watt's descendants are off somewhere, completely unaware that they are super-intelligent?" asked Megan.

"I suppose so," John paused, sipping his tea and nibbling a chocolate digestive. "Of course, while the responsibility is always passed down, the actual superpower isn't always needed, so sometimes it lies dormant for generations. Like your parents, for example."

"Wait," said Cam, pointing at John and then back at himself, "we have the same powers."

"That's right," said John, shuffling uncomfortably. "I'm guessing that you must be the son of Mildred's girl?"

"Mildred, my gran..."

"Right. Well, I'm Mildred's big brother."

There was a long pause. Cameron looked like he really wasn't up for this news. "She never mentioned a brother," he said.

"Well, she wouldn't," said John darkly. "I ran away y'see. Relatives didn't talk as openly about things in those days. Anyway... happy families!"

John attempted an awkward side-hug. Cam patted John on the shoulder, looking like he would rather be anywhere else in the world than so close to John's coat.

"So what relation does that make you?" Megan laughed.

"Great-uncle Catman," said John, "the black sheep of the family. Quite literally, if required."

"Is that everything?" asked Cam. "Or does it get even worse? Is TJ my second cousin or something?"

"Almost everything," said John. "When your gran and I were growing up, there was a big fuss about the river being contaminated, because of all those strange fish washing up on shore. This new company turned up in town..."

"Clutha Chemicals?" said Megan, pointing excitedly to her newspaper clipping.

"Yes. They tested the water, then they tested all the children in the town, 'for our protection,' they said. That's how me, your gran and the others all met. Jimmy told us all the story I've just told you, helping us understand what was happening and find our way as guardians."

"Why was TJ there?" asked Cam.

"On a government placement," said TJ. "Mr Watt donated me to the government to do classified work. That's why I helped in the world wars, and then after that, top-secret cover ups – such as children being tested for 'exposure to lethal chemicals', who were really being tested for 'abnormal abilities'. When their powers were detected I knew they must be guardians like me; I helped them escape."

"Who were the others?" asked Megan.

"Tam Ash and Hannah Glass."

TJ's eyes flickered. "Ash, Stone, Glass, Bone."

"And Tin," said John, tapping TJ's head, "don't forget Tin."

TJ stared. "I am... trying."

"I know," said John, "sometimes I wish I could forget too."

# CHAPTER 28...

It was a cold clear early evening, and up on the moor, away from all the streetlights and houses, the stars were all the brighter. Megan couldn't stop herself from flying up towards them.

"This is beautiful!" she said, floating on her back, staring up into space.

"It is, but that's not why we're here. Tonight is all about stealth," said John. "Yes you should run towards trouble when your help is required, but you also need to be able to move between places unnoticed, quickly and carefully. I want us to get from up here down to the river's edge at Lunderston Bay without being seen."

"Does that include TJ?" asked Cam. "Only that squeaky wheelbarrow we sometimes have to push him round in isn't very ninja."

"I am invisible to radar," said TJ.

"Are you invisible to eyes?"

Megan shushed them both as she glided back down.

John tapped TJ on the shoulder. "You get a head start, Jimmy," he said, "and it's that way, remember?"

TJ nodded and then began slowly plodding back down the hill.

"Right Megan, do a few loops and we'll give you a head start too," said John. "There's something I need Cam to try."

As Megan whirled above them, John turned to Cam. "It's good that you can change into different animals now," he said. "You can imagine much more than when we started."

"Thanks." Cam blushed slightly; compliments were usually something that happened to other people.

"But if you want to avoid turning into a grumpy old man living in a cave," he glanced over to where Megan was laughing and spinning weightlessly, "and if you want to help her, then there's more to do."

"Ok," said Cam carefully, "like what?"

"You need to move with the landscape, become part of it."

John gestured to Megan, who was flying upwards in a graceful spiral. "She understands it perfectly, without even thinking. So did Sarah. It's harder for you and me. But we can do it."

"You're the boss," said Cam.

"Ha," said John, "I'm not the boss of anything. Never have been. I'm not even the boss of myself any more.

That's what this power can do to you if you're not careful."

"What do you mean?"

"I don't stay in a cave because it's cool, Cam."

"I dunno. Peace and quiet, no one bothering you. Seems great."

"I stay up there so I don't scare or accidentally hurt people. You saw what happened the first time you and Megan came in. The more time I spend as an animal, the less human I can be afterwards. It's addictive being an animal – you've felt the rush – but it's a lonely thing to be forever. And I don't want you to ever get like that."

Cam nodded slowly and John gave him a pat on the back.

"Ok. Before we change, let's take a few minutes to listen quietly to what's around us."

Cam nodded, and listened.

"Can you hear it?" asked John.

"What am I listening for?"

"Everything. The motorcycle on the hill miles away, the lambs bleating and running..."

Cam was frowning, concentrating hard. "I can hear Megan breathing up in the sky! That's amazing! Animals under the ground digging, water running downhill!"

"Good," said John, gently. "Now, let's run."

Megan watched as Cam and John turned into rabbits and bounded across the open fields, weaving over bogs and marshes, following the water downhill. She realised she had just lost her head start and, laughing, flew after them.

At the lochside, without pause, two rabbits dived in, turning effortlessly into trout and plunging down through the reeds.

Next they splashed out of the loch onto the muddy shore as frogs, leaping twice into the long grass before sliding swiftly onwards as snakes. When they reached the tree line, they scuttled into the forest as squirrels, leaping from tree to tree, freefalling then catching the next branch. And the next one. And the next.

Out from the forest onto the roadsides, they each ran on four legs, canine paws pounding the pavement, a blur of grey fur against the grey tarmac. On and on, running down the hill. The wide firth of the River Clyde lay ahead, and with it new sounds: the scuttle of crabs in rockpools, the frantic paddle of gulls' feet beneath the surface of the water, the banging of a boat engine. And something else – a pounding, rhythmic thud. TJ was close by too.

The two animals slowed, finally allowing themselves to stop.

Megan floated down to join them. "Cam! When did you learn wolf?"

Cam lay on the shale, growls turning gradually to laughter as he became himself once again. "My superhero name is totally going to be Wolfman," he said. "That was amazing."

"There's nothing like it," said John. "Well done, both of you."

John waited until Megan flew upwards again before he whispered, "Just remember, the more you do it, the harder it is to want to turn back. Make sure you always have a reason to keep *two* feet firmly on the ground instead of four."

"No worries. I'd miss TV and biscuits too much," said Cam.

"Yeah, that's what I used to think."

John shut his eyes for a moment, thinking something over. "Megan, TJ," he called, beckoning them to where he and Cam were sitting, "let's head back to the cave. I think it's time I told you both what happened the last day my generation of guardians were all together – the day Clutha Chemicals won."

Out on the river, the little boat Cam had heard puttered on, out towards the islands.

In its wake, a girl bobbed up and down in the icy-cold water. She watched the strange old man, the flying girl, the tin man and the wolf-boy turn back along the coast towards the lights of the town.

She wanted to shout out, to swim towards them and say hello. Instead, she waited until they were out of sight and spun the waves around to push herself up onto the surface. Then she walked across the waves towards the shore alone.

# CHAPTER 29...
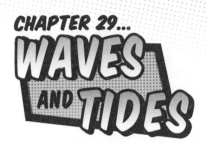

Back in the cave, John was rifling through his bookshelf. He lifted an old leather-bound book from underneath a little statue of Sarah's monster Gorskyn. He opened the book and took out a black-and-white photo that had been tucked inside it. He passed it to Megan.

The photo showed four smiling teenagers standing on a hillside. Tin Jimmy was saluting next to them.

"That's my gran," said Megan, singling her out immediately, "and you, John... and Hannah and Tam?" asked Megan, pointing at the two she did not recognise.

John nodded, and looked at TJ. "Have you remembered it all yet, Jimmy?"

TJ looked at the picture, staring intently at the two. "I remember her laughter, his jokes. I remember... it all went wrong..."

"Yes," said John, "sounds like it's coming back to you."

Cam pointed at the photo. "What went wrong?"

"Hannah liked to call herself a water witch," said John, appearing to ignore Cam's question and gently taking the photograph from him. "She could control waves, swim like a fish. A right wee mermaid. Tam had invisibility."

"And what happened to them?" prompted Megan.

"Thanks to Jimmy, we knew Clutha Chemicals were after the power under the water. Watt built his shield almost three hundred years ago; for all we knew, Clutha Chemicals would be able to smash it open with modern equipment – they had somehow got their hands on a submarine. So we weren't just trying to hide the sigils, we were trying to stop them getting that sub near the power at all. We knew we were in danger of death or capture, so Sarah made sure the sigils were all hidden somewhere new, somewhere even we didn't know about in case we were questioned."

"And were you caught?" asked Cam.

"Clutha Chemicals knew we were coming before we even got there. We fought long and hard – we destroyed the sub – but Hannah and Tam went down with it. Hannah could hold her breath for a long, long time, but not that long."

"Wait, what?" asked Cam, genuinely shocked and now much more worried than usual. "Just like that?"

"Just like that," said John. "It's not something I like to talk about. Fortunately there isn't anyone out here to tell." John winced as he said this, and stripes rippled across his face.

"I... remember..." said TJ slowly.

Megan and Cam stared at one another in silence. For the first time since unfolding the letter from her gran, Megan didn't want to know any more, didn't want all the answers, didn't want to be involved.

Cam leaned forward. "Wasn't there anything you could do?"

"We were still in terrible danger. Sarah had been swept away by the current – I didn't know if she was dead or alive. Jimmy and I ran from there to Port Glasgow and the bomb shelter where we agreed we would hide him if things went wrong. Then I ran too. The people on the submarine had all seen me, but they hadn't seen Sarah. I had to get away to avoid getting both of us in trouble. I ran for the hills. And I've been hiding ever since."

John looked at TJ guiltily. The robot was as blank-faced as ever.

"It was worse for Sarah though. I ran away from the world, but she had to stay in it. Hannah and Tam's deaths and my disappearance were covered up as a big local tragedy of course. There was talk about river contamination being to blame, but most folk thought Hannah and Tam and I were just some unlucky kids caught in the currents. Life moved on. Clutha Chemicals closed down in 1966. No wonder really. They'd lost their sub, killed off most of the guardians and lost the sigils too. Things were quiet for a long time until earlier this year when I first felt it again, the fizzing in my chest... I always thought that was the thing under the river calling out to us, pulling us into action. And that's how I knew it was going to start again, that the guardians would waken."

"There are five," said TJ quietly.

"I can't believe Gran had to deal with all of that and never told anyone," said Megan.

John coughed awkwardly. "It took Sarah a long time to begin living a normal life again. I think it helped her to tell stories, write fantasy books – all those river monsters and shape-changing werewolves."

Megan looked at the old photo again, at the smiling friends in their early teens who had no idea what was going to happen. "I wonder who our other two are," she whispered.

John went to place the photo back inside the book. "So y'see this is why I want you both to be ready. More ready than we were." He shook his head sadly. "I don't want to lose anyone else."

"Hold on a second..." Cam was looking at the newspaper, really squinting at it. He set the clipping down on the ground and took out his mobile phone, snapping a photo.

"What are you doing?" asked Megan.

"Look more closely at the picture," said Cam. "Doesn't one of those doctors look a little familiar?"

Megan picked the clipping back up and peered at it, while Cam was zooming in on the photo on his phone. The photo was a little blurry, but even if Megan had not been able to recognise the man from the photo, she could read the name badge he was wearing.

"Professor *Finn!*" shouted Megan.

"So yeah, maybe Clutha Chemicals disappeared," said Cam, "but it looks like someone is carrying on the family business."

"Makes sense," said John. "We need to find those sigils before they do."

"Oh good," said Cam, "because number four on the map is a graveyard."

# CHAPTER 30...

The old cemetery had not been used since the end of the nineteenth century. People still died after that, of course, but there was no more room to squeeze them in, so a nice new cemetery got built somewhere else instead. Now parts of the old one were being carefully dug up and moved to accommodate a new Bingo hall.

Cam was waiting for Megan and TJ at the cemetery gates. "Why would anyone demolish a graveyard?" he said. "That's got to be bad karma."

Megan stared at the portacabins and portaloos nestled alongside the ancient stones. "So... what do we reckon then... zombies or ghosts? Based on our luck so far?"

"I think we have enough *real* stuff to worry about, thanks," said Cam. "Like my mum finding out I'm not really on the basketball team. Or in the chess club. Or singing in the school show..."

"Yeah... my parents are expecting me to be crowned Maths Champion of the World with all the extra work I've been doing..."

"Ghosts are very real," interrupted TJ, surprising them both.

"What? Don't be ridiculous. Dead people floating about everywhere?" Cam waved his arms around to make his point.

"Not dead people. Memories, emotional recordings impressed upon objects. I see the playback."

For a moment, nobody spoke.

"Your robot's broken," said Cam. "It's seeing things."

TJ clapped a rusted hand on Cam's shoulder and pointed into the graveyard dusk.

"Over there is a little girl crying at an old graveside. The grave is of a boy. He died very young. The girl cannot see us, is not really there. The stone, the soil, the trees, have all recorded her emotional response, the many days she wept here. I see the playback."

"But... but there's no one there," said Cam, genuinely peering across the graveyard.

TJ clicked, whirred and turned to Megan. "Your friend is broken. His eyes don't work right."

Megan once again reminded herself that TJ was a robot and not an actual person. "Is that how you heard the children whispering at Crowfell?"

"Maybe," said TJ, "or maybe I remembered them from when I was there."

"So, where are we supposed to be looking? Does your gran want us to start digging up random graves?" asked Cam.

"I don't think she'd make us go that far," mused Megan. "What about in there?" Megan pointed to an ornately carved stone structure near the far wall.

"The crypt," said TJ. "Crypt first."

"And... just to check," said Megan, "are you... seeing anyone at the crypt right now?"

TJ studied the back wall intently. "No."

"Ok then," said Megan. "Let's go."

"I wish your gran had left you a map of chip shops," said Cam.

TJ pulled at the crypt gate hopefully. "Locked."

"You know what we need," said Megan, smiling, "a skeleton key."

Cam just scowled at her.

"I have burned out the lock," announced TJ. "There is no key required."

The gate creaked open in exactly the sort of way Cam hoped it wouldn't, and they stared down the steep stairway that descended underground.

"This probably isn't the time," said Cam, "but I'm not totally sure what a crypt is. Is it, like, where they store all the garden tools and lawnmowers?"

Megan quickly silenced TJ with a look. "Uhm... yeah," she said.

At the bottom of the stairs, a carved wooden door opened into a small room.

176

"Bit posh for a shed," said Cam.

"Look at the carvings," said Megan, "they're really weird."

In place of the cherubs, angels and roses traditionally found in cemeteries, the carvings on the crypt door included skeletal knights, sea monsters, flying horses and crows.

"Cheery," said Megan.

"Not much room for gardening stuff in here," said Cam. "What are all these name plates for?"

For a moment it was quiet enough in the crypt to hear a penny drop.

"Crypts are actually where posher families would all get buried together," said Megan quickly, which she hoped would make it easier for Cam, like when you rip off a plaster.

"We're in a *grave*!" shouted Cam, backing towards the stairs, then turning around with a start just in case there was a vampire walking down, on his way home. "People are buried in here! Right here!"

"Do not worry Cameron, they pose no current threat." TJ patted Cam reassuringly on the arm. "There. There there."

"Doesn't this seem like the most likely place for a hidden sigil Cam?" asked Megan.

"It seems like the most likely place for a horror movie."

"It's so sad," said Megan, tracing her fingers across the

engraved lettering of the name plates. "So many of them died really young. Wait. This one says Watt – it might be a clue!"

**CATHERINE WATT**

BORN 1791
DIED 1680

"Hold on a second... She died one hundred and eleven years before she was born?" said Cam. "That's a hard life."

TJ reached out to touch the plate, and it fell from the wall.

Cam squealed, "Are there bones behind it?"

TJ took the remaining brick carefully from the wall and examined it. "There is some writing carved onto the brick, but it is hard to make out."

Megan took it from him, while TJ stuck his hand without hesitation into the gap left by the brick.

"TJ, don't do that!" said Cam. "Something could grab you."

"There's something else written here," said Megan. "I think this says 'ill'?"

Cam knocked the brick out of her hand. "Plague grave. It's a plague grave. Let's get out of here!"

TJ pulled his hand from the wall. "I cannot reach all the way in, but I am sure there is something there. A smaller hand could reach."

Megan sighed. "Of course it could." She took off her glove and began rolling up her jumper sleeve.

"Cameron's hands are smaller," said TJ.

"No, it's ok," said Megan, "I'd only have to do it anyway after he fainted. But Cam, seriously, if I get grabbed by a skeleton you'd better turn into a dog and start hunting for bones."

"I just don't like dead things," said Cam. "That's actually one of the more normal things about me."

"TJ was right!" Megan's arm was now deep inside the wall. "There is something here!"

"Is it something with teeth?" asked Cam.

"Got it!" Megan pulled her hand out. She was holding a small leather pouch, tied with what looked like old shoelaces. She carefully untied the bag and tipped the contents into her hand. The sigil was slightly grubbier than the other two had been, a bit scratched, but there was no mistaking that they had found what they were looking for.

"Excellent," said Megan, "now we have two out of three!"

"Great news," said Cam. "Can we go now?"

"You're already halfway up the steps so we might as well," said Megan.

CHAPTER 31...
BELLS AND WHISTLES

As they emerged from the crypt, coloured lights streamed across the tombstones, illuminating the graveyard and casting long shadows. At the cemetery gates was the source of the light show: a large, mostly spherical sculpture. Pale reds and greens beamed eerily from its interior.

"It's Evolve," hissed Cam. "I didn't know it had lights inside it."

"Yes, very pretty," said Megan, "but I don't think it's here to go disco."

Megan turned to TJ, quickly opened his chest cavity and threw the little leather pouch inside. "Remember TJ, you get back to John even if we don't, ok?"

"I remember," said TJ, "though I am not pleased with this plan."

"Me neither," said Cam, "but we don't have enough time to come up with a new one. Come on."

Cam and TJ ran around the back of the crypt while Megan flew upwards to give herself some room. Evolve swivelled, following Megan's flight, silhouetting her against a night sky of red and green.

"It's just like taking a run up," Megan told herself. "Just like a long run up to a big jump."

She breathed in and swooped down towards Evolve as quickly as she could, balling her hands into fists, and aiming for the smallest sphere in the centre of the robot. Megan connected with Evolve, generating a clang that sounded like a bell chiming. She was so surprised she hadn't broken her arms that it took her a few more seconds to realise she had actually knocked Evolve over.

There was a loud ringing in the graveyard, and Megan turned towards the portacabins, worried that they had accidentally set off a security alarm. The noise seemed to be all around them. Evolve's lights spun wildly, beaming out across the graveyard, lighting up TJ and Cam who were clambering over the wall.

With horror, Megan realised she was hearing an alarm clock.

Clock-faced Chronos was waiting for Cam and TJ on the other side of the wall, behind the crypt.

Luckily, Cam had spotted the robot on his way over the wall and transformed instantly. This time he was more creative, knowing how strong Chronos had been at Crowfell Hospital. He became a mouse and scurried through the grass towards the sculpture.

The sculpture could tell something was not right. It began thrashing out at its own body when it felt the little creature climbing up its legs. Mouse-Cam scampered higher, creeping along the clock hands before finding a tiny gap he could squeeze through at the top of the robot's head. Cam took a quick moment to catch his breath, his tiny heart racing.

He wasn't sure how he had expected the inside of a robot's head to look, but it seemed quite empty, with the exception of a few microchips, wires and a tiny black aerial. The aerial was attached to a bulb that flickered green and angry red.

Chronos figured out where Cam had disappeared to, and began banging and shaking his own head. Inside, Cam started to feel worse than the day he was seasick on the Rothesay ferry.

By the time Megan had flown over to help, Chronos had removed his own head and was furiously rattling it. Cam fell to the ground and transformed back into himself, looking slightly green.

"Cam! Quick, get up, come on!" Megan shouted.

While Chronos secured its giant clock head back on its shoulders, Evolve began moving again, despite being slightly wobbly. It weaved between gravestones, heading straight for the wall, as though it would crash through onto Megan and the fallen Cam.

TJ decided to lead Chronos off in a random direction. While this would mean leaving Cam and Megan behind, they'd at least have only one robot to deal with. What TJ had not factored into his calculations was that Chronos was much quicker than he was. The sculpture grabbed him and they tumbled down into a wide ditch of recently opened graves, soon to be the foundations for the Bingo hall.

"Cam, can you change into anything?" said Megan, panicking. "Anything at all, even a mouse again?"

Cam didn't reply. Evolve rolled ever closer.

"Cam seriously, come on!" said Megan.

Without speaking, Cam managed to change – a tiny gecko lay on the grass.

"I hate lizards," said Megan, scooping him up and gently putting him in her jacket pocket. "Did you do that on purpose?"

Megan flew back over the graveyard, where she could see TJ struggling with Chronos. "TJ! Catch a hold," she shouted.

"I cannot," said TJ, looking up to see Megan sweeping across the ground towards him.

Megan grabbed TJ by the arm, and together all three of them flew away from the graveyard back towards the hills. Megan's training had helped – her flying was stronger than it had been before – but soon the weight became too much. When she was sure they were far enough away, she lowered TJ and the gecko to the ground.

"I am sorry, Megan," said TJ. "It is my fault."

"It's not your fault," said Megan, "we just didn't expect two of them, that was silly. But we made it!"

"No, the mission failed. Chronos took the sigil from me."

"What?!" Megan was unable to hide her upset. "When?"

"When we fought in the hole in the ground. I was trying to get it back when you grabbed me."

"So... that was all for nothing!?"

"I am sorry, Megan."

Cam groaned. "Listen Meg, I know you don't want to hear this right now, but you probably need to throw this jacket out, unless you want to stink of gecko sick."

Relaxing claws
for stress-free
destruction.

Gentle rolling motion for
no-hassle chases.

EVOLVE

# 32. TOYS AND GAMES

Chronos lay twitching in the opened graves. Mr Finn had decided to watch his sculptures in action again this evening, and had noted of a few modifications to assist with future battles. This time, any dents and bumps had been worth it.

"It's a terrible thing," said Mr Finn, clambering down into the grave. "Most people just don't appreciate great art. But I do."

He took the little leather pouch from the sculpture and examined the sigil.

"One for them, two for me," he said. "Y'know, these guardians have a bad habit of letting their guard down."

Mr Finn started whistling 'Don't Stop Me Now' by Queen (which he liked to imagine was his own evil theme tune), hauled himself out of the grave, and headed home.

The laboratory was jam-packed with evil that day. The final sculpture, Kevin's sea monster Destiny, was almost complete, and Mr Finn was still working on Resilience's weaponry upgrade.

"What do you think? Time to move house? Getting a bit cramped in here."

Resilience shuffled awkwardly in agreement, his spikes grazing the walls.

"And we need somewhere to fix Chronos now as well… hmmm. What about that old Gaelic church in the town? I was going to send you to knock it down… but it might be just what we need right now. How are you getting on?"

Resilience pointed to a collection of dangerous-looking objects on a bench. Mr Finn picked one up and pulled the trigger. A purple laser blasted a massive hole in the wall.

"No!" said Mr Finn angrily. "No, no, no! That's completely the wrong colour. It shouldn't be chill-out purple, it should be angry red! If we use this to melt a building everyone will laugh. It's embarrassing."

Resilience looked down at his jaggy robot feet.

"And as for this disintegrator cannon… it looks like it's been made out of Lego."

Mr Finn threw the cannon onto the floor angrily,

where it immediately smashed, because it *had* been made out of Lego. Resilience looked sheepish.

"This is serious. I left strict instructions for you. We're supposed to be getting ready to destroy superheroes, not having fun."

Mr Finn picked up the final item on the bench and pushed a button. A fizzing electrical net sprang out and fired across the room, pinning Resilience to the wall and paralysing him under the current.

"Hmmm," said Mr Finn. "Ok, that's actually pretty good."

He walked over for a closer look at the new sculpture. "And Destiny's coming along nicely. Looks comfortable enough inside."

Trapped and sparking behind the electric net, Resilience's eyes flashed.

"Not long to wait now," said Mr Finn.

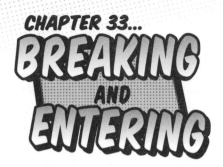

# CHAPTER 33...
# BREAKING AND ENTERING

Cam and Megan didn't talk about their graveyard misadventure the whole way through school the next day. Neither of them wanted to think about the most difficult bit – how they would explain losing another sigil to John. That's why, even though they had to endure double PE, equations, extra washing-up in Home Economics, and cheese-and-spinach pie for lunch, the day still slipped by faster than ever.

Megan found Cam waiting at the gate and they both sloped off to see John, or 'after-school homework club', as they liked to call it at home. He had a cup of tea and extra chocolate biscuits on the table for them – even for Cam – when they arrived.

"TJ told me everything," he said as soon as they walked in. "Sounds to me like you did brilliantly. You were just unlucky."

"But we lost the sigil," said Megan.

"It was mostly my fault," said Cam. "I got dizzy and threw up. That wasn't very super."

"It was me who lost the sigil," said TJ. "Cameron disrupted Chronos from the inside and Megan knocked over Evolve with a flying punch. It was most impressive."

"Sounds it," said John. "Think about what you did well; don't focus on where you think you went wrong. Even a few weeks ago you wouldn't have been able to do what you did last night."

"I suppose..." said Megan, "but what do we do now?"

"Well," said John, "even before last night I was wondering what to do about the sigil Waterworx already had. So while you were busy at the graveyard, I went on a wee mission of my own."

"What sort of mission?" asked Cam.

"I went to look at the Waterworx offices," said John. "Seems to me that all we need to do is break in and steal the sigils straight back. Finish up your biscuits and we can get going."

It was the first time Cam and Megan had smiled all day.

The Waterworx offices down by the docks were shiny, expensive and mostly empty. One or two employees were still milling around, about to clock off for the day.

Big important-looking banners hung in the high windows, each displaying one gigantic word:

# VISION

# FUTURE

# INNOVATION

As if having the words hanging up in the window was enough to make them true.

"How is this going to work?" asked Cam, self-consciously looking straight at the CCTV camera, then turning quickly and guiltily away. "I've never broken into a building before. It's one of the few things my mum can be proud of."

John shook his head, smiling. "It's not like breaking in at all. No smashed glass, no alarms. I go places all the time, no one ever notices."

"How?" Cam asked again.

"Did you know that in Britain you are never more than three metres away from a rat or mouse?"

Finally Cam understood, "That's why you've been making me practise mouse again?"

John nodded. "Hamsters can be a wee bit too chunky to fit through all the pipes and cracks."

"So what's the plan then?" Megan asked.

"To be as quick as possible, since the statues seem to turn up wherever we are, but I'm hoping they won't arrive while people are still hanging about." John glanced at the front doors of the office. "Best way in? Always round the back by the bins."

Not only was it quieter round the back, but the doors were still open because the workers had been smoking outside.

"Filthy habit," said John. "Right, Cameron and I will slip inside and find a place where we can see the staff setting the alarm. Megan and TJ, you stay in the shadows back here. We'll let you in once we've deactivated the alarm."

John and Cam shrank, almost disappearing, before scuttling quietly inside through the open door. Cam followed John, who stuck close to the walls, running along skirting boards and ducking under sockets and cables. He stopped under a desk at the front of the office. Feet clattered by the glass door, a forest of shiny black shoes and sharp-looking heels. There was laughter, doors slamming, more footsteps and then four beeps before all the feet finally disappeared through the front entrance.

All was quiet.

Cam was just about to go exploring under people's desks looking for crumbs, when he saw John change back.

John turned to look at Cam and shook his head. He then pressed the same pattern of buttons on the alarm panel until there were four beeps again. This time, he gave Cam a thumbs up. "I'll go let Megan and Jimmy in."

"Aren't we supposed to wait until it's properly dark or something?" asked Cam.

"No time for that," said John. "Besides, if anyone looks in now, we just appear to be people working late. Get seen wandering around buildings late at night – that's when you look guilty."

"Isn't TJ a bit conspicuous to be in a big building full of windows?"

"Nah," said John, "he can stand right near the door and keep a lookout. Folk will just think he's one of the company's daft statues." John shuffled quickly through the office and out to the back door, returning with Megan and TJ.

"That was a bit easy," said Megan warily.

"Lots to do before we can say that for sure," said John. "Let's make this quick. Downstairs, five minutes max."

"What's downstairs?" asked Cam.

"Usually the stuff people don't want you to find," said John.

"And you think the sigils will be here?" said Megan.

"I know they will be – I watched Finn all day yesterday," said John.

Beneath the gleaming offices was the basement of a much older building. Crates were stacked high along each wall, archaic numbers and indecipherable squiggles scribbled on them.

"Over here," said John. "Look!" He pointed to a desk and lamp tucked away between some crates. The desk was scattered with old newspaper pages, comics, yellowing letters and photos – all of them about Tin Jimmy.

"Someone is very interested in your robot," said Cam.

A tin robot-shaped piggy bank stood under the lamp. John picked it up and rattled it. A sigil coin fell out, catching all of them except John by surprise.

"What we have here," said John, as he examined it, "is someone who knows the price of everything and the value of nothing."

"To be fair John, we did just break into his office," said Megan.

John had also picked up a little leather pouch beside a box of highlighter pens.

"That's the one from last night!" said Megan.

Carefully tipping the coin into his hand, John smiled. "This one was mine." He passed the sigil to Megan, and stroked the bag between his fingers. "My dad made me this wee bag for taking money to school. I haven't seen it for years." As if it were the most precious treasure, John gently tied the little pouch strings together and placed it in one of his many pockets.

"Ok, this has gone well; three–nil to us now," said Cam. "Let's quit while we're ahead and get out of here."

"TJ and Megan should take a sigil each for now in case Cam and I need to change," said John. "Plus, that way we've split them up if there's any trouble."

"Shouldn't we take all this stuff about TJ?" asked Megan, pointing to the files spread out across Mr Finn's desk.

John was carefully placing the robot piggy bank back where he had found it. "It might take them longer to figure out someone's been here if we don't. Cam's right, let's just go before a sculpture catches up with us."

# CHAPTER 34...

# FUR AND FEATHERS

Outside, Megan carefully shut the back door. "Oh wait," she said, "did you set the alarm again?"

"Why would I do that?" asked John. "They are the baddies, I don't care if they get burgled."

"Plus I've forgotten the code already," said Cam.

"Two nine zero nine," said TJ.

John, Cam and Megan all stared at him.

"Grease and dirt signatures on the most-used buttons," he said, tapping his eyes by way of explanation. "After that it's just a matter of variables. And I am finding those much easier to work with since Megan's upgrade."

"So," said Cam, frowning, "why did we bother going in the back way as animals then?"

"Oh," said TJ, "I thought you could use the practice."

"Anyway," said John, quickly changing the subject, "we got what we came for, so..."

Megan was no longer paying attention to the conversation, she was looking over towards Civic Square, where the Phoenix Egg sculpture had recently been installed.

"Uhm," she said, "I think the statue's hatched."

The others followed her gaze to see the ornately crafted steel eggshell, unfolded like an opened Chocolate Orange.

"I *knew* there was something in there," said Cam.

"Yeah, so the big question is, where has it gone?" said Megan.

The answer arrived suddenly from above. Something swept at TJ, metal talons screeching against his tin skin, before it shot upwards again.

"Bird robot," said Megan, as the sculpture settled clunkily on the Waterworx roof above them. "Makes sense."

"Quick!" John pushed Megan and Cam away from the robot towards an alleyway, and TJ marched out towards the square. Wings outstretched, Phoenix squawked and shrieked at him. Flames burst from its beak.

"TJ!" shouted Megan.

"This is his fight," explained John. "Neither of you are fireproof, so stay out of it."

"No, he needs help!" Megan struggled to get past John.

"He's fought wars against Napoleon and Hitler. I think he'll be fine."

Megan quickly looked around the narrow alley where they were protected from the flames. The sides of the

PHOENIX EGG

filthy buildings climbed towards the sky. She glanced back at Cam and John.

"Sorry," she said, and flew straight up into the evening clouds.

Everything looked prettier from above. Grey streets softened into patchwork, making everything seem like it was in the right place, part of some larger pattern – except the bit that was on fire.

Steam and black smoke billowed upwards from the riverside as Tin Jimmy and Phoenix clashed. It was difficult to make out the fight properly, but it didn't look like TJ was winning. Phoenix just kept sweeping upwards and flying down, talons out, flames blasting at its prey.

The sculpture, however, wasn't thinking about what might be above it. Megan dived down, landing hard upon its back. She began pulling at its head from behind, yanking at the beautifully sculpted metal feathers.

This certainly got its attention; it spun around and upwards, spiralling through the air, desperately trying to shake her off. Megan held on for as long as she could, but when she fell, instead of dropping towards the ground, she pushed further up, fairly sure that Phoenix wouldn't be expecting that. She was absolutely right. This moment of confusion gave her enough time to launch herself once again at the sculpture's head.

Megan summoned every ounce of strength she had, genuinely hoping she might be able to knock its head off entirely. She stunned the sculpture enough to knock it down towards the ground, where she could now see that TJ, a gorilla and a polar bear were waiting to help.

Megan and Phoenix crashed onto the cobbled dock, the statue's outstretched wing slicing a nearby bench in two.

"Hold the mouth!" shouted Megan to John. "Stop it fire-breathing."

She scrambled back as the polar bear clamped its mighty paws around the sculpture's beak while gorilla-Cam sat on its feet.

TJ, meanwhile, was busy searching through the metal shell Phoenix had escaped from. "I think I have it," he announced, tearing a huge handful of wires out from inside the eggshell. In the tangled mess of cables, Cam spotted the little red and green light he had seen inside Chronos just as it flickered out. There was a strangled squawk and Phoenix stopped moving.

Megan stared quickly around Civic Square. Amazingly, no one had responded to the commotion yet, but they wouldn't have long before the fire brigade turned up to check out the smoke. "Is everyone ok?" she asked.

TJ walked over and hugged her, his tin skin still hot from Phoenix's flames. "Thank you Megan."

"You're welcome," she smiled, "but we'd really better get out of here."

The polar bear pointed back towards the alleyway they

had originally been hiding in, then loped off towards it. He had already hauled up the drain cover by the time the others reached him. Turning back into John, he issued a hoarse "Follow me" and lowered himself down into the drain.

"Great," Cam said. "I was wondering what could be more fun than breaking and entering."

He, Megan and TJ splashed into the dark after John.

Out by Civic Square, hidden from view, Kevin quietly replayed the footage he had just filmed on his mobile phone. Massive wild animals smashing up statues? It was just too good not to share.

# VANDALS TRASH TOWN'S NEWEST SCULPTURE

ANOTHER one of the new sculptures installed in the town as part of a redevelopment scheme has been badly damaged by vandals.

Last month we told you how abstract sculpture 'Resilience' had been stolen and then smashed in an evening of destruction which also resulted in the demolition of the Tobacco Warehouse, one of the oldest buildings in the town.

Today we reveal that Civic Square's new statue, Phoenix Egg, had a surprise inside – a surprise that has now been ruined for the public.

The sculptures were designed and installed by the Waterworx company, which has been rejuvenating parts of the town with new offices and a series of public art sculptures. Company director Mr Finn explains, "The idea was that the egg would hatch at the official unveiling of the sculpture, and inside, a beautiful Phoenix would announce its arrival with specially rigged fireworks."

But before this could happen, Phoenix Egg was smashed open and the sculpture dragged onto the street where it was badly damaged. Mobile-phone footage from the evening of the attack apparently shows two men dressed in gorilla and polar-bear suits, who were responsible for the incident.

In the last six months the town has seen a spate of often irreparable damage both to new and old monuments. We must surely now ask if this is part of an organised campaign of civic vandalism.

# CHAPTER 35...
## TWO AND THREE

After the footage was shared across every phone in the town, it was more important than ever to maintain a low profile. Luckily, the shaky recording didn't start until Megan and Phoenix had already crashed to the ground, so she wasn't visible in the film. Unluckily, that did make it look like John and Cam were just battering a helpless sculpture rather than defending themselves from a terrifying, fire-breathing robot bird.

The weird thing was, when they all watched the film back at John's cave the next day, the gorilla and polar bear *did* look unrealistic. Perhaps it was because they seemed so out of place in the town square, your brain just forced it to make sense. All the same, it gave them something to think about. So when stories also started circulating about a wee boy who claimed a flying girl had saved him from drowning, well, it was time for a talk.

"I can't believe Richard didn't mention me," said Cam. "I was the one who actually pushed him out of the water. Unbelievable. This must be how Robin feels all the time."

"I am not Batman," said Megan. "We do need to be more careful not to be seen though."

"This is why I think we should have costumes," said Cam. "Or at least you should when I'm disguised as an animal."

"He's right," said John.

"Yes," said Megan, "because crazy colourful superhero outfits will work like camouflage."

"Look, even if it's just a mask for now, Megan, you really should think about it," said John. "It's just safer that way."

"It seems silly," said Megan, "like we're playing a game or something."

"Well, we aren't," said John. "If people know who you are, they can find out who your family are too."

Megan thought of John, hiding away from his family for years just to keep them safe. Suddenly a mask didn't seem quite so silly.

"But we're winning!" said Cam, trying to lighten the mood a bit. "We have three sigils and we know where the fourth one is." He pulled out his phone and showed John his digital map. "The final place to go is the old Sugar Sheds. Unfortunately, that's where they're putting the last sculpture, so there'll be a robot waiting for us."

Megan was frowning. "There are five sigils, though," she said. "That's right, isn't it John?"

"Yep. Five sigils. Five guardians. And we've only got three of each."

"So how come we only have one place left to look?"

"We could do with more guardians as well," said Cam. "That way we could maybe take on one robot each."

"Yeah. There should be a water person like Hannah and an invisible person like Tam."

"Great, it should be really easy to find someone invisible," said Cam.

A sudden beeping made them all jump.

"Morse code again," said TJ, tapping his chest.

"Any change to the message?" asked Megan hopefully.

"No," said TJ. "Still incomplete."

"I really wish we knew who that was," said Cam. "Maybe they have the other sigil. Do you remember yet who might be contacting you?"

TJ suddenly began banging his head with both of his metal hands. "What. What. What."

"TJ! Calm down!" said Megan.

"What. What. What?" There was a small pop and a few sparks, then TJ was silent.

"He's gone funny again," said Cam. "I thought your upgrade was supposed to stop him malfunctioning every time he got a Morse-code message."

"I thought so too," said Megan. "Maybe he got damaged by Phoenix. Hang on." She took a screwdriver from John's shelf and carefully unscrewed the plate at the back of the robot's head.

"Cool," said Cam, "he looks much more interesting on the inside."

"I was a bit worried that the solar panel might not be a good idea with our weather," said Megan. "Perhaps he needs a back-up power source. Are you ok, TJ?"

"What. Yes. I... I... I..."

"We're sorting it TJ," said Megan.

Cam was peering inside the back of the robot's head, looking slightly worried. "Meg, what's that?" He pointed to a large microchip connected to a little bulb that was flashing red and green.

"Dunno," said Megan. "That microchip is one of the older pieces. Every time I tried to disconnect it, he completely switched off. It was wired to the Morse-code machine originally."

"Right," said Cam, "but you fixed that?"

"Well, there's still a connection, but the Goozberri Five is the main control now."

"Ok," said Cam, "it's just that Chronos and Phoenix have the exact same bit inside them."

"What? Seriously? TJ, do you know what this chip is?" asked Megan, tapping it.

Sensing her hand inside his head, TJ moved it slowly from side to side as if trying to crack his neck.

"Yes," said TJ, "communications from Finn."

"Finn?!" said Megan. "What do you mean? You speak with Mr Finn?"

"There are five," said TJ.

# CHAPTER 36...
# HEROES AND VILLAINS

There had never been a more awkward silence, and considering how rude and tactless Cam could be, that was really saying something.

"Finn! Mr Finn?!" shouted Cam angrily. "From Waterworx?! The bad guys!"

John looked horrified. "What does this mean? Have you been spying on us?"

Megan stepped in front of the bewildered robot, firing a warning glance at John and Cam. "No. He wouldn't do that to us."

TJ clicked and whirred in confusion. "Megan, I do not understand."

"It's not your fault, TJ. It's not your fault," said Megan.

"Yes it is his fault, Meg," said Cam. "*He's* why the sculptures keep turning up wherever we go!"

John was holding his head in his hands. "TJ, how

long have you been in contact with Mr Finn?"

"Professor Finn reactivated me in 1953. It was forgotten. Until now."

John was shaking, and patterns of fur were rippling in waves just under his skin. Cam could see he was struggling hard not to become a wild animal, to lash out. "I can't believe this Jimmy. The day of the submarine attack... That's how they knew we were coming... You were our friend..."

"He *is* your friend," said Megan. "He couldn't help it."

"Mr Watt built me to protect," said TJ. "I protect."

"Well, you didn't protect Hannah and Tam!" roared John.

Cam quietly stepped beside John, just in case he had to move quickly to stop him.

"You just do what you are programmed to, you can't help it," said Megan.

"I do not want to," said TJ, still shaking his head. "It was forgotten."

TJ stood, clicking and whirring as he tried to find a way for it not to be true.

"Professor Finn must have known you were a guardian and reprogrammed you to find the others and act as a double agent," said Megan.

"I did not know!" whirred TJ. "I would not harm."

John had slumped into his chair. "Some guardians," he said. "We were leading the bad guys to the sigils all along."

"Not quite. You did it right, especially when Gran hid them herself," said Megan. "You kept the sigils safe from Professor Finn. We just have to get all the sigils before his son finishes the job."

Megan spent the next hour fiddling with the wires behind TJ's tin skin, while John and Cam sat wordlessly in the shabby makeshift living room.

"It looks like Professor Finn's rewiring made TJ send a regular signal displaying his GPS location."

"So that's how they always know where we are?" asked Cam.

"Yes," said TJ, obviously once again dismayed at having put his friends in danger. "I am sorry. I did not know."

"Remember there was beeping as soon as we switched TJ on? You thought he was a bomb."

"Well, he did blow up my shed," said Cam, "so I'd say I was half right."

"There is a second function," said TJ. "The Morse-code link allows two-way communication. I am programmed to respond."

"And have you?" said Megan.

"I have sent no functional messages since 23 May 1965."

"The day of the submarine attack," growled John.

"I think you have been fighting it, TJ," said Megan, "even if you don't remember."

"Is that why he goes all haywire whenever he receives the message?" asked Cam.

Megan suddenly got so excited she started hovering. "This is brilliant!"

TJ, Cam and John all looked at her, clearly not seeing how brilliant it was at all.

"Mr Finn can track TJ, right? And that means we've been leading them to the sigils this whole time.

"That explains why they haven't tried harder to actually kill you..." John grumbled.

"Yes, and if we've been leading them *to* the sigils..."

"We can lead them the wrong way too," said Cam. "We can send TJ somewhere else while we go and find the fourth sigil!"

John smiled for the first time in hours. "You're both even smarter than my lot were, and there are only two of you. Sarah would have been so proud."

"But it gets better," said Megan. "We know Mr Finn can contact TJ, but he doesn't know we know. Y'know? So we should pretend we don't know."

"Ok, I'm lost now," said Cam. "And actually I think I've been doing pretty well."

"Mr Finn keeps sending TJ the Morse-code signal but TJ hasn't responded," said Megan. "If he does respond, maybe Mr Finn will send him specific orders..."

"And we'll know what he's up to!" said John.

"I do not want to help them," said the robot, sounding as near to annoyed as it was possible for him to be.

"You won't be," said Megan. "They will just think you are. You can be a decoy. A double agent!"

"Will that help to fix things?" asked TJ.

"My gran used to say that if it's not broken, don't fix it." Megan smiled and hugged the robot. "Though to be fair, she actually did break quite a lot of stuff."

"But what if Mr Finn finds out... what if it goes wrong again?" said TJ.

"You're forgetting something else TJ," said Megan, opening TJ's chest plate to access the Goozberri Five now installed inside. "We've been reprogramming."

John smiled. "Ok then, sounds like we have the advantage. Let's finish this. Better late than never."

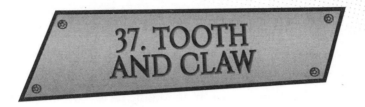

# 37. TOOTH AND CLAW

It was an unusually glorious winter day at the Sugar Sheds. Mr Finn took a moment to survey the sunshine, and smiled. He couldn't care less about the sun of course, but the good weather meant that more people than expected had turned up to see the fifth and final sculpture unveiled. There were lots of parents and teachers accompanying hordes of uninterested children. The local press were out in force too – the unveiling was now big news, thanks to the high-profile damage to the other sculptures.

"Probably hoping some monkeys and bears turn up to push it over," thought Mr Finn, not totally sure himself that they wouldn't.

The statue was draped in a gigantic blue flag with the wavy Waterworx logo printed across it. Mr Finn didn't like blue, but the board wouldn't let him change the

Waterworx colours to black and red. "Too sinister," they said, entirely missing his point.

These were the exact same people who had refused his suggestions for electric fences and desk-mounted flamethrowers to ensure office security. If they had just let him dig that big pit full of spikes or fit the Autostomper into the ceiling, maybe the office wouldn't have been burgled. Or if it *had* been burgled, it would be full of crispy, squashed burglars.

Mr Finn tried not to think about the waste of all his hard work finding the sigils, and did his best to smile.

He looked like a skeleton with stomach cramps.

Kevin, who had won the school design competition, was waiting to pull the cord and unveil his creation. And of course get his grubby little paws on a free Playstation.

All Mr Finn hoped was that this sculpture would be terrifying enough to deter superpowered vandals and burglars. And if some babies and old ladies in the crowd got a fright and started crying too, that would be a bonus. He stepped up to the microphone and showed his teeth.

"Thank you very much for coming along to support us today," he said. "I know we've been unlucky with our lovely sculptures in the last few months, but I'm certain this one could hold its own in a fight."

There was some nervous laughter in the crowd, but not much. Clearly none of these idiots had a sense of humour. Mr Finn pushed on.

"And a special thank you to Kevin here, who designed this wonderful creation. Kevin, would you like to do the honours?" He pointed at the cord.

Kevin pulled, dragging the Waterworx flag away to reveal a majestic sea serpent coiled around a fountain. Each metal-plated scale shone in the sun.

"Ladies and gentlemen, meet Destiny!"

The sculpture's teeth and claws sparkled most of all.

There was some genuine applause this time, which caught Mr Finn a little offguard, so he pushed Kevin forward to the microphone. "Tell them where you got the idea from," he hissed.

"The sculpture is based on a monster from one of Sarah Stone's books," said Kevin. "A friendly river serpent who lived in the Firth of Clyde."

"Yes," said Mr Finn, snatching the microphone back from Kevin. "We were all saddened by the death of local author Sarah Stone last year. This is our way of paying tribute. Although, this is obviously a much less friendly serpent; it would likely have your hand off."

Mr Finn glared at the crowd severely, just in case any more wannabe superheroes happened to be hiding in there, considering causing trouble or stealing things from his offices.

"So, thank you one and all for coming along today," said Mr Finn. "A small selection of reasonably priced refreshments are available from the snack van across the street. Enjoy."

DESTINY

People stared dutifully at the statue for a few seconds more, making all the sorts of sounds and noises you are supposed to make, while Mr Finn waited. He was not going to leave his beautiful new sculpture alone until everyone had gone. To encourage them along, he decided to make another announcement: "Please do not let children sit on the statue as it is razor sharp. It would be awful if anyone ended up horribly injured."

That seemed to do the trick.

Mr Finn had not been in the best of moods since the Waterworx office break-in. Even firing all his employees hadn't cheered him up. Neither had inventing gelignite marshmallows. It helped a bit to unveil the huge killer robot today, but he was still feeling glum. So his plan for the night was to go back to the office, do a little more tedious investigating of Watt's old documents, then go home to his lab. He wanted to trial some of Destiny's remote-control systems, possibly smash some stuff up too. With any luck, that would help him figure out what was going wrong with his attempts to control the Tin Jimmy.

Every time he sent his father's master control signal, he received a burst of complete gibberish back. For a while he'd thought it was coded messages, but he couldn't decipher a thing.

He was beginning to wonder if he had misunderstood his father's notes.

His fingers were black with newsprint ink, his eyes ached from straining to read. So many months of digging through boxes, scanning old newspapers, cross-referencing the notes his father had left, ransacking abandoned buildings and stalking children to find every scrap of information about Tin Jimmy or the guardians or the river. He was sure he was missing something.

And it turned out he had been.

As I approach my final days, I think often of my robot guardian and of the system I devised to lock away the secret power: only all five sigils applied together are able to unlock the shield beneath the river. I continue to hope that the four other guardians keep their sigils hidden and safe, however, I ensured a final failsafe to protect the power. The fifth sigil is a disguised key, and no one except myself and my robot know its location...

It is the robot itself. He is the final piece, his hand is the key. Each of the other four sigils must be slotted into place first to allow his hand to unlock the shield beneath the river.

If he is lost, no one will ever be able to unlock the power. As long as he functions he will continue to protect the town: an eternal guardian programmed to obey only myself, the four others, and our descendants for evermore.

This will be my final diary entry. My work is done.

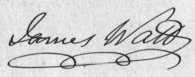

Mr Finn almost jumped up and down with glee when he read this. But then he remembered he was supposed to be a serious villain, so he just nodded, stroked his chin and did an evil laugh in front of his mirror. It wasn't very convincing, so he practised it a few more times until it sounded right.

The *robot* was the last sigil. It all made sense now. Finn had never fully understood why the robot had been such an important part of his father's plan. Hacking in and taking the place of James Watt as his master, creating the control signal, setting a trap for the guardians: it was all in order to gather the sigils. His father was much smarter than he had given him credit for. Although that didn't stop him being a rubbish dad.

Mr Finn now had all the pieces in place too. And, unlike his dad, he had five gigantic robots to help him open the shield and unlock the power for himself.

Now Mr Finn's laugh sounded exactly right, but it was interrupted by a beeping from the other side of the room. It was the Morse-code machine. Mr Finn went over to check, expecting nothing more than the random selection of letters and numbers he usually received. This time, however, there was something much more interesting in the code:

.. / .- -- / .... . .-.. .
I    am     here

--- .-. -.. . .-. ... / .--. .-.. . .- ... .
Orders      please

# CHAPTER 38...
# SUGAR AND SPICE

Megan woke up early the next Saturday, feeling as if it were Christmas, only instead of elves and presents, there were going to be giant robots and explosions.

She reached for her phone to text Cam, but it beeped just as she picked it up.

> Morning. Can't eat breakfast. H8 giant robots.

Everything had been planned and arranged. All they had to do was wait for the pieces to fall into place. Sure enough, as soon as Tin Jimmy had sent that message to Mr Finn last night, he received instructions to come to the Gaelic church today at noon. That was the starting pistol.

They met up with John earlier than usual to go over the plan.

"This is perfect. Finn won't be expecting us to look for another sigil while TJ is occupied elsewhere," said John.

"I will stall Mr Finn for as long as possible and tell him I know where you have hidden the sigils," said TJ, "and offer to take him there."

"While in fact I will have all the sigils," said Megan. "And we will be sneaking past Destiny at the Sugar Sheds to get the next sigil."

"And where will you take Finn, TJ?" asked John.

"To the bomb-shelter tunnels in Port Glasgow, very slowly," said TJ. "And by the time we're back from the Sugar Sheds," said Megan, "we will trap Mr Finn and any sculptures that have followed us in the tunnels."

"There are lots of confined spaces to get stuck in," said John. "We just have to block the entrance."

"Easy. What can possibly go wrong?" said Cam, sarcastically. He had already gone through all the things he was pretty sure *were* going to go wrong. The list started with *I fall in the freezing river* and finished with *Waterworx have an army of flying monkey clowns and they're hungry.*

"I still wish we knew if the other guardians are out there somewhere," said Megan. "Maybe they could help."

"Maybe," said John, "or maybe they'd get hurt because they haven't had weeks of training."

Megan wondered if they would feel it – the fizzing in their chests that she and Cam felt now – dragging them like magnets towards the fight.

"Good luck everybody," said John.

Megan gave TJ a hug.

Despite their rather cute name, the Sugar Sheds were not made out of candy bricks and peppermint cobbles, they were gigantic red-brick monoliths left over from the once-booming sugar trade. There were five interconnected sheds in total: two had been cleaned up and turned into offices; the other three were stuffed with junk.

"There's Destiny," said Cam, pointing. "Looks... scarier than the others."

"Well, you helped to design it," said Megan. "Well done."

The three of them clambered over the rear wall beside the boats, then slipped along the back of the massive building, out of the robot's sight. However, Destiny's eyes briefly flashed red and green.

"I don't think the sigil is actually in the sheds," said Cam. "The number on the map is on the docks in front."

"There's an underwater walkway," said John. "My dad was a docker. He said there were a few tunnels that served as shortcuts between the sheds and the docks."

"That sounds like the sort of dark, dank place we've come to know and love," said Cam.

"Let's take a shed each and look around," said John. "We're probably after a trapdoor or something."

Cam sighed, already fairly sure he was going to find the trapdoor first, just as soon as he'd fallen through it.

Inside the sheds, there was a stickiness to the air, and to the floor – a faint smell of candy apples and molasses mixed with petrol and damp.

"This is lovely," said Megan. She brushed against a wall and got covered in bird poo and brick dust. "I think Sugar Sheds may be too nice a name for these."

Scaffolding and rickety rusted-steel stairs hung from every wall, daring the unwary to climb. Megan was wary though, so the scaffolding was wasting its time.

"Over here," hissed John, his whisper echoing around the empty sheds. He had lifted a steel hatch on the ground, revealing a set of steps that plunged sharply downwards.

"Yeah, that looks about right," said Cam, as he came over, his nose wrinkling at the stale air that rushed out of the hatch. "And it smells right too."

Megan and Cam began treading down the stairs, occasionally steadying themselves against the wet walls.

"I'll stay here," said John. "I don't want us all down there if the hatch shuts."

Cam whimpered a bit. "Can I have the big torch then?" he said. "For once I actually miss TJ with his big light bulb eyes."

John tossed the torch to him. "Be careful," he said, "and be quick."

At the bottom of the stairs, the walkway stretched off into the dark, far enough that even the big torch couldn't find the end. Little puddles were dotted before them, moisture splashing gently down from the ceiling.

"Ok," said Cam, "I think we should just run over to the other end really fast with the torches on full beam, then quickly work back."

"Agreed," said Megan.

Together they splished and skiddled through the damp dark, torchlight throwing strange shadow shapes on the walls as they ran. When they reached what had looked like the end of the tunnel, they were disappointed to find that it was a junction, with two equally damp and dark tunnels stretching off to the left and right.

"We should split up," said Cam. "You take left and I'll take right."

"What, really?"

"No! Are you mental?"

Megan smiled. "Let's try left first."

At the far end of the tunnel was an old ladder leading to a steel door in the ceiling, which had been welded shut.

"It was a brick in the crypt, so maybe it's a brick in here too," said Megan. "Let's check the walls for anything unusual." She shone the torch onto the wall – the entire tunnel was built of red bricks.

"We can't check every single one, there's thousands of them!" said Cam. "Also, if you pull bricks out of an underwater tunnel... doesn't water get in?"

"I suppose," said Megan. "Ok, let's try the other one."

Down the right-hand tunnel was a massive steel door, badly rusted and firmly shut.

"Do you think it's behind here?" said Megan, pushing at the door. "Because I'm not sure how we can get this open."

"What if we both charge at it?" said Cam. "If I go gorilla and you go back down the tunnel, take a run-up, then fly at it, full speed."

"We might bring the whole place down," said Megan.

"Well, if that happens," said Cam, "you'd better be ready to fly back out carrying a gorilla."

Megan disappeared back along the corridor, as gorilla-Cam began to push. With a whoosh and a smash Megan flew into the door. It crumpled and gave way in a shower of brown dust, and they tumbled together into the next section of tunnel. They held their breath as a single solitary drop of river water dripped down from the ceiling above.

In the space behind the door was another ladder leading up to another welded door.

"This is useless," said Cam, shaking dust from his hair after he had changed back into human form.

Megan was staring at a rusted sign which had been screwed onto the wall behind the ladder. It said 'In Case of Emergency'. She turned to her friend and whispered,

"Cam, help me get this sign off the wall."

It didn't take much effort to loosen the sign; it slipped down on one side, hanging by a single persistent screw and revealing a loose brick in the wall. A brick stamped 'IV'. Megan reached over and pulled it from the wall.

Megan took the sigil coin out. "Four–nil," she said, smiling. She threw the brick to Cam.

"Four. Wait a minute," he said. "Four! IV is roman numerals for four." He turned the brick so Megan could see.

"Oh yeah, that's clever."

"No. Don't you see? It really is! Each sigil has been marked with roman numerals! The brick in the crypt didn't say 'ill', it said three – roman three. III."

Megan suddenly understood. "Five is V," she said, hopping on the spot. "That Morse-code message! U.R.V. You are five!"

Cam's mouth dropped open. "TJ isn't just the fifth guardian, he's the fifth sigil! You are five!"

There was a distant clang, the terrifying but un-mistakable sound of a steel hatch slamming shut. Then, from above and echoing all around them, they heard an awful metallic squeal like something rusted being forced open.

"Cam?" said Megan, knowing something was badly wrong, but not yet sure what.

And then water blasted into the tunnel from the river above.

# 39. LOOK AND LEARN

The Tin Jimmy moved carefully: quick then slow, always along back roads and in shadows, or under the ground in forgotten sewers and aqueducts.

Mr Finn followed at a discreet distance, just in case it was a trap. "Secure the fifth sigil," he repeated to himself under his breath, over and over again.

He felt confident. There were Waterworx security guards in the old Gaelic church waiting to capture the robot. Once the fifth sigil was properly under their control, getting the others would just be a matter of time. And Mr Finn was a patient man.

The Gaelic church was just ahead, as abandoned as all the old buildings in this horrible little town. It was being used by Waterworx as an 'art workshop' to restore and repair the Phoenix sculpture, since Mr Finn's house was getting pretty full.

The robot entered the church. Mr Finn gave it a few moments, then casually wandered in behind it.

Inside, the Tin Jimmy lay on the floor, twitching and sparking under the electric net that had just been dropped on top of it.

"Tin Jimmy! Oh I've been wanting to meet you for ages," said Mr Finn. "I would have arranged a chat sooner, but you haven't been taking my calls."

"There are five," said the robot.

"So I gather," said Mr Finn, "though possibly not quite that many now…"

The Tin Jimmy's light bulb eyes flickered. "What do you mean?"

"Your friends, the superhero guardians? I'm afraid I've had to stop them causing trouble. Permanently."

The robot's eyes now flashed angrily. "Impossible. You do not know where they are."

"Of course we do. They are at the Sugar Sheds getting the last sigil," said Mr Finn. "When I worked out that all the sigils had been hidden in old buildings, I put the oldest buildings in town under surveillance. It's not hard when your company's main job is knocking down old ruins to build new office blocks."

"What have you done to them?" asked the robot, struggling to move under the net.

Mr Finn looked at his watch. "Well, it was a stroke of luck that last sigil being at the docks right by Destiny. And Resilience, Evolve and Chronos are on their way there too. Just to be sure. It's a shame it has to end like that. If no one had got in our way, we could have found the sigil coins without anyone getting hurt. So actually, if you think about it, it's their own fault."

The Tin Jimmy shuddered angrily. "You are mistaken."

"I suspect you were supposed to be a diversion today," said Mr Finn, "but actually, it turns out we need you *more* than all the other sigils anyway."

The robot blinked silently, the net sparking and fizzing against his metal body. "What do you need me for?"

"Well, *Jimmy*," said Mr Finn, "don't you know? You yourself are the key that all the other sigils need to work. Finally I can finish the job my father started, with or without your cooperation. You see, technically, we don't need all of you, just your hand." He gestured to a large workbench where there was a circular saw.

If Mr Finn had been listening properly, he might have heard a small gasp from one of the darker corners of the church. Kevin had heard enough. He had been watching and following Mr Finn since he saw the Phoenix sculpture come to life. Kevin didn't understand everything he'd heard, but he knew it wasn't good. Nice people didn't threaten to cut up friendly robots who hung out with Cam and Megan.

Somehow, he was going to have to help without Mr Finn seeing him.

So it was really lucky that Kevin could turn invisible.

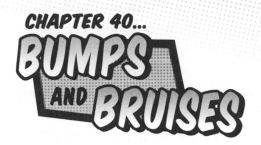

# CHAPTER 40...
# BUMPS AND BRUISES

Cam had transformed the moment he heard the first splash. It was the only way he could be sure to get Megan out.

It didn't seem like so very long ago that he had dived into the dam and could only turn into an otter. This time he knew exactly what the situation needed: fast, powerful, dangerous, shark-Cam torpedoed under the fast-rising water and found Megan. She was a little surprised, but Cam decided to take that as a compliment.

Megan grabbed a fin and braced herself for what she knew was coming. They could see the hole that had been smashed in the tunnel above, allowing the water to pour in. It wasn't big enough for them both to fit through. So, together they charged back towards the closed steel hatch, which was now totally submerged. If they were going fast enough, and if the water pressure was on their side, they might be able to smash it open. If not, they were very likely to get splattered. Either way, it would be quick.

Cam swam up the staircase they had walked down less than half an hour ago and pummelled into the hatch. It gave way with a rusty shriek. Megan let go of his fin and tried to find her balance, but she was dizzy and her soaking wet clothes were heavy. Cam lay gasping in a puddle, changing back so he could breathe.

It had all been so scary and sudden that it took Megan a few moments to look up and realise that they were still in trouble. Polar bear-John was desperately trying to fight off the combined strength of Resilience and Evolve.

"Cam!" shouted Megan. "Gorilla!"

Without even turning around or getting up out of the puddle, Cam changed. Within seconds he had jumped on top of the freshly repaired Resilience. Megan flew at the beaming madness of Evolve to try and distract it from John, who she now saw was hurt. One of his front paws hung limply by his side, and his white fur was streaked with red. Evolve had clearly not fared much better – many of the sculpture's internal spokes were badly bent or snapped entirely. It would not take much, or at least that's what Megan hoped as she spiralled up into the shed's rafters.

Evolve followed, clambering up the scaffolding on the back wall. Megan waited until it was almost at the top, then swooped towards it. Evolve lunged at her, grabbing uselessly at the space where she had been. Now off balance, the sculpture teetered and wobbled; it took only a swift kick from Megan, now sweeping in from behind, to topple it entirely.

With a crunch, Evolve smashed into the dusty cobblestone floor and was still.

Megan could see that Cam was holding his own against Resilience, so she flew to John, who had changed back to his human form and was slumped against one of the steel posts that supported the building.

"John, we need to get you away from here. Can you walk?"

John shook his head. "I'm not going anywhere; we're not done here."

Megan could see he was holding his side with his one good arm. "Are you ok?"

"Did you get the sigil?" he replied, ignoring her question.

"Yes... and we figured out where the last one is. It's TJ; he's not guarding it, it's *him*. You are five. That's what the Morse-code message meant."

There was another crash and a brief shower of brick dust as gorilla-Cam swung Resilience around and bashed him into a wall. Resilience, at last, stopped moving.

"Hah. I suppose TJ forgot that too," winced John. "Sarah must've expected him to tell us. She always did have a bit too much faith in that machine. Well, you'd better go get him then. Cam and I have got this covered." John winked unconvincingly.

Megan sighed, knowing John was worse off than he was letting on. "Three guardians isn't enough. There should be five of us."

"It's ok, Megan," said Cam breathlessly, once again human. "You've got all the other sigils. We can finish this now if you go get him."

Megan looked at her best friend, exhausted, wheezing and pale, then at John, broken and bleeding. Resilience and Evolve lay smashed and shuddering in the dust. She knew she had to take this chance.

"I'll be quick," she said, "promise."

As Megan shot out of the warehouse doors and up into the blue, John smiled at Cam. "I hope you've had a big breakfast," he said, "because we're not done yet."

Behind Cam, at the dockside, Destiny hauled itself out of the river, having failed to get rid of them by flooding the tunnel. Hundreds of metal scales tore into the resurfaced concrete walkway as it snaked over to them.

At the other end of the sheds, an alarm bell signalled the arrival of Chronos.

"Oh," said Cam, "excellent."

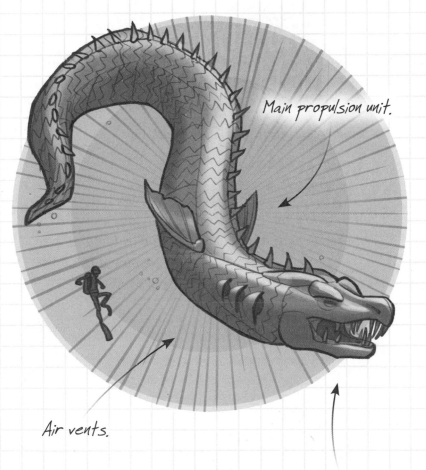

Main propulsion unit.

Air vents.

**DESTINY**

Enormous jaws.

CHAPTER 41...

# FRIENDS AND FOES

Megan had never flown so quickly, driven by fear for her friends back at the dock, and for what she was about to find. Something felt wrong. She had gone to the tunnels first, where TJ was supposed to lead Mr Finn, but there was nobody around. The Gaelic church was straight ahead now, and she hoped to find TJ standing outside with a captured Mr Finn. "Some Finn bothering you?" she had planned to say.

But nobody was waiting outside the church. Now, certain something bad had happened, she flew straight through one of the many smashed windows – and stopped in mid air. TJ lay on the ground beneath a wire net. Megan was so shocked by the sight of the crackling net over her helpless robot, she didn't notice the Waterworx guards standing just below her.

"Megan," said TJ, trying to struggle free of the net.

But it was too late, the security guards had grabbed her feet. There were too many of them holding on for her to fly away. Mr Finn stepped out from the shadows.

"Hello Megan," he said. "Best tie her to something very heavy."

"What have you done to TJ?"

"Nothing to worry about. I certainly don't want to damage the fifth sigil."

Megan's face fell. How could *he* have known when they hadn't?

"Now Megan," said Mr Finn, "I'm guessing that you have the sigil coins I need. Once you've given me those, Tin Jimmy and I will take a trip under the river to unlock the shield Watt created. And I'll claim my superpowered reward."

Megan was barely listening; she was watching TJ twitch and shudder under the net. "You're going to break him! Take it off. Please, I'll give you the sigils! Don't hurt him."

Mr Finn gestured to his security guards. "Take off the net. He's under my control now anyway."

Megan watched as TJ was released. He stood slowly up, head and limbs still jerking slightly from the current. Mr Finn flipped open the panel at the back of the robot's head.

"Leave him alone!"

"I was quite impressed at your handiwork," said Mr Finn, looking inside. "You completely bypassed the command chip my father installed."

"TJ was never his to control."

"Oh really?" Mr Finn held up the severed Goozberri Five cable. "See for yourself."

TJ's eyes flashed green and red in response to Mr Finn's voice.

"Now, where are the sigils, Jimmy?" asked Mr Finn. "Do you have them or are they hidden down some other rabbit hole in this miserable little town?"

"They are in Megan's pocket," said TJ.

"Could you fetch them for me please Jimmy?"

TJ walked to where Megan was tied. She squirmed away from him. "TJ, don't do this. You're a guardian, remember? This isn't you."

"He's not a guardian," laughed Mr Finn, "he's a robot. *I'm* the guardian. Inventing has always run in the family, y'see. From me and my beautiful killer sculptures all the way back to James Watt and his... steam-powered tin man. Haven't you guessed, Megan? I'm Watt's great-great-great-great-grandson. And I'm sure we can all agree I am pretty great." Mr Finn knew that gag would have gone down a storm with a better audience.

"So you see, the robot, the sigils, the shield, the superhuman powers... it's really my birthright."

"If you're a guardian, you must already have superpowers," said Megan, still not wanting to believe it. "Why bother trying to unlock Watt's shield?"

"I do," said Mr Finn, tapping his head. "Super-intelligence. Just like Watt. And being a genius is all very well, but sometimes you want a little something more.

Hurry up Tin Jimmy, time to go."

Megan couldn't look at TJ as he reached into her pocket and removed the four coins. She was speechless.

TJ handed the sigils to Mr Finn, who smiled sarcastically at Megan. "Don't take it personally. He's just following his programming. He's on the same control network as all my robots now. Phoenix!"

In the corner of the room, Phoenix stood up and stomped towards them.

"On you get, TJ," said Mr Finn. "You and I are off for a trip 'doon the watter', as I believe they say round these parts."

Megan watched helplessly as Mr Finn and TJ clambered onto the sculpture – until she felt a tugging at the ropes that tied her to some huge pipes.

"Shhh!" hissed a voice. "Stay still."

Realising someone was helping her, Megan tried to distract Mr Finn. "TJ won't let you do it. I know he won't."

Neither the robots nor Mr Finn noticed her moving as the giant bird began to launch itself off the ground. Megan threw herself towards Phoenix with all the force she could manage, but its massive wing struck her across the head, knocking her back to the ground.

Phoenix, with TJ and Finn on its back, smashed through the old church roof and into the sky.

The Waterworx security guards were still staring upwards through the massive hole in the ceiling, so Megan seized another opportunity. She flew at them, knocking them unconscious against the wall. "Ok," she said, turning around. "Who's there? Who helped me?"

Megan let out a small piercing scream as Kevin immediately appeared in front of her. She stepped back in surprise.

"Kevin! Did you... can you...?"

Kevin nodded. "Flying's cooler though," he said modestly.

"Not from where I'm standing," said Megan, smiling. "I cannot believe we didn't notice!"

"Yeah well," said Kevin, "I've always been especially good at not being noticed."

# CHAPTER 42...

# HEADS AND TAILS

Up close, it looked much better than Cam had imagined it would. The sculpture he and Kevin had designed was actually rather beautiful, each scale individually crafted, glimmering like oil on water, throwing little rainbows across the cold stone floor. Although of course, as it turned out things would have been easier if they had gone with the stupid sugar cube idea instead.

Destiny loped towards them, and without thinking, Cam stood in front of John, ready to protect him. "John, can you change? You need to run."

"I'm not leaving you," said John.

"No, I was going to run too," said Cam. "I just thought it was polite to let you go first."

Cam glanced at the other toppled robots. Evolve was still not moving, but he could see the first sparks and flickerings that indicated Resilience was gathering strength.

"John, we need to move," Cam whispered.

Then there was a sudden crash and a shower of glass and brickwork as Phoenix smashed through the Sugar Shed roof and slammed down near Destiny. The serpent immediately stopped advancing on John and Cam and stood to attention alongside Resilience.

Mr Finn and TJ climbed down from Phoenix and walked quickly towards Destiny. John and Cam stood still, unsure of what was going on.

"You'll forgive me for not stopping," said Mr Finn, pointing what looked like a set of car keys at Destiny, "only we're in a hurry."

"TJ!" Cam shouted, but the robot walked straight past him.

There was a beep, and then a side panel on Destiny slid open, revealing seats and a large control panel. Mr Finn and TJ climbed inside. As he went to slide the panel shut Mr Finn looked up at the giant bird. "Phoenix, finish them off please. Resilience, Chronos, with us." The serpent turned and sloped out of the sheds, splashing straight into the river while the other two robots stomped behind.

"Uhm, what?" said Cam.

Phoenix stepped towards them, preparing for attack.

Cam was just wondering if he could somehow change into an elephant, when Megan swooped through the hole in the ceiling and smashed into the robot. Caught offguard, Phoenix shook and then toppled. It writhed and slipped on the ground, unable to get up onto its skinny bird legs.

"Megan, what's going on?" said Cam. "I feel like I've missed something. Lots of things actually."

"Finn's controlling TJ, he's related to James Watt, he took all the sigils off me, and they're going to unlock the gate."

"Seriously? You were only away about ten minutes!" said Cam.

Kevin appeared next to Cam, smiling. "I know! It was crazy!"

Cam's face went white.

"Oh... and I brought Kevin with me. He turns invisible," said Megan. "He's our number four!"

"Kevin?" said Cam. "That's just great." Happily the only person this fooled was Kevin.

"Just one more to go then," said John, standing up carefully and keeping an eye on the thrashing Phoenix.

"Well, we don't have time to wait," said Megan. "You two need to get under the water and stop Finn. If you can force Destiny back up, Kevin and I will attack from above."

Cam looked at John. "Meg, I'm not sure if..."

"I'm fine," said John, "let's go."

Unconvinced, Cam followed John to the river's edge and together they dived into the cold black water, transforming as they went.

"What can I do?" said Kevin.

"There's lots of wee dinghies and smaller boats over at the marina," said Megan. "Any chance you could go invisible and 'borrow' one?"

Kevin grinned. "Brilliant." He climbed down onto the marina walkway.

He didn't see the girl out in the water, watching him. With a ripple, she turned and dived beneath the waves.

# 43. TOIL AND TROUBLE

Under the water, Mr Finn made the best of his head start. The sculpture-sub was already approaching the impact point of the meteorite, as shown on his father's maps. While TJ steered the sub, Mr Finn was struggling to get into his atmospheric diving suit. It was a lot harder than it looked, but only the robot had seen him get tangled up and fall over, so it was totally fine.

As he and TJ emerged from the sub, he was struck by how horribly cold and dark it was under the river. It was difficult to see more than a metre or so ahead. However, he could make out the dark shapes of Resilience and Chronos already scanning the area for the lock. Watt's notes had a few early design sketches of the piece, but no pictures existed of the finished device. Luckily, Mr Finn had brought someone who knew exactly what it looked like.

TJ walked slowly but purposefully along the riverbed towards a circle of rocks and seaweed beside Resilience. Mr Finn watched as TJ cleared away the seaweed and barnacles to reveal a huge rusted metal panel. It was covered with ornate circular symbols. This was it. The lock.

Right in the centre of the panel was a large round indentation with five smaller circles, presumably where the robot would put his hand and fingers. Around this circle, at each of the compass points, were four gaps that he guessed corresponded to the sigils.

*Beautiful craftsmanship*, thought Mr Finn. *What a total waste to stick it underwater.*

Mr Finn gestured to TJ, who nodded and slowly began pushing the sigils into the four compass points. As each one clicked into place, a little column of green bubbles burbled out from the riverbed in front of them. Mr Finn then pointed at the largest circle. The robot hesitated, just for a moment, before placing his hand into the grooves of the panel.

After a few seconds of nothing happening, his eyes flashed green. He moved his hand a quarter turn to the left, then all the way over to the right. There was another flurry of bubbles, and the darkness that had surrounded them began to shimmer with an eerie luminous green glow. The glow was coming from a crack that had started to widen in front of them, like a huge eye slowly opening after centuries of sleep.

Oily green and purple bubbles began to rise slowly towards the surface, like the thick blobs inside a lava lamp. Mr Finn stared into the growing gap, unclipped some sample tubes from his diving suit, and began catching bubbles. TJ stared at the rising bubbles. He reached out to touch one and it burst, sending green liquid sinking back to the riverbed.

Then all the bubbles started bursting, and they were lost in a swirl of purple and green as a shark and a killer whale rammed into Resilience and Destiny.

CHAPTER 44...

HIGH AND DRY

Shark-Cam swung back towards Mr Finn, who was floating above a massive chasm in the riverbed. He saw the panel with the sigils slotted into it, and realised what had happened.

*He's opened it, we're too late*, he thought. Cam tried to peer through the bubbles at what lay behind Watt's shield. Before he could get a closer look, a huge jagged arm swept down towards him. Resilience was slower under the water, but that didn't make it any less strong. John, only a few metres away, turned and blasted through the water like a torpedo towards Resilience, throwing all of his strength into his attack. The robot shuddered, allowing Cam to swim out of the way. However, the impact had been too much for John, and Cam watched in horror as the old man changed back into his human form and sank, unconscious, to the bottom of the river.

In the churning chaos caused by the fighting, TJ was still striving to protect Mr Finn, and so had begun dragging him, struggling, back towards the lopsided sub.

Cam also turned back to his human form, as he couldn't think of any other way to move John. *Must work out how to do Octopus*, he thought, *or merman.*

Chronos stared at the toppled Resilience and continued marching across the riverbed towards them. Cam couldn't hold his breath much longer. He didn't think he'd be able to carry John up to the surface and deal with Chronos while he was at it.

*Maybe I won't get a chance to do octopus after all*, he thought.

Just as Chronos was almost upon them, it wobbled and shuddered as if the ground was shifting beneath it. A black shape swam quickly around the sculpture, darting in between its grasping arms and stomping feet. Sand and silt from the riverbed began to rear up: a huge tidal wave of dirt slowly overwhelmed Chronos. The robot toppled and sank beneath the silt, buried to the waist.

That was when Cam saw the girl. She was wearing a wetsuit, but no mask. Weirdly, that didn't seem to stop her from breathing. She smiled and waved briefly at Cam, then pointed upwards. She began twirling the pointing finger, and all around them, the water began to swirl and churn.

*She's controlling the water*, thought Cam. *She's our number five!*

Carried by the girl's current, Mr Finn, TJ, John and the Destiny submarine floated to the surface. As they all rose, the girl swam to John, and took both his arms before shooting upwards, leaving only bubbles in her wake. Cam was swept up after them, and burst out of the water gasping for breath.

Above the water, Megan had already grabbed Mr Finn and hauled him up into the sky. She looked angrier than Cam had ever seen her – and Cam had made her angry more times than anyone else. She dropped Finn into a small dinghy below, where a rope began tying itself around him.

Kevin gave Mr Finn a few seconds to scream with terror before he appeared. "Only me," he said, waving the end of the rope in his hand.

"Meg, it's too late," shouted Cam, "it's open. All this weird colourful stuff is leaking out."

But Megan wasn't listening. She had spotted the girl, who was struggling to keep John afloat. John was coughing and spluttering, but at least he was breathing. She flew down to help.

"So our number five turned up!" added Cam.

"You are kidding!" Megan laughed and turned to the girl. "You're here just in time...Water powers, right?"

"Yes but..."

"Awesome! Back in a minute." Megan lifted John from the water and flew back towards the dockside, seating him against one of the few walls that were still intact.

"Are you ok?" asked Megan, because that's the first thing you say to people when you know they aren't.

"Few wee bruises," said John, coughing and spluttering. "I've had worse."

"I'm so sorry I asked you to go down there."

John shook his head and waved away her concerns. "Look, it's not over yet. You guardians need to lock the shield back up. We have no idea how dangerous all the stuff that's leaking out is."

"I know. We're all here now. We can do this." Megan squeezed John's hand and then flew back out over the river.

Cam, Kevin and the water girl had managed to get TJ into the dinghy, but he was inactive. Megan hovered above the surface of the water and smiled again at the water girl who had rescued her friends.

"Hi again. I'm assuming Cam hasn't done introductions 'cause he's really rude," said Megan, reaching out to shake the girl's hand. "I'm Megan."

"Lily," said the girl, smiling.

"Hi Lily. I'm not sure how you're here, but I'm really pleased you are. We have *so much* to talk about, but right now it would be great if you and Cam could get back under the water and try to lock the power back up..."

"The big crack that all the glowing bubbles are leaking from," explained Cam, "just next to where you sunk the robot."

"Right," said Lily. "Uhm... how do we do that?"

"I'll show you when we're down there," said Cam.

"And while you're doing that, I'll try and fix TJ," said Megan, "because he needs to get down there as well to close it properly."

"This is the best day ever," said Kevin, tying Mr Finn's knots just a bit tighter.

"You ready Lily?" asked Cam.

Lily nodded, and began sinking bank under the river. Cam began his transformation into a seal, and seconds later they were gone.

Megan opened the panel in TJ's head and water slooshed out everywhere. The same thing happened again when she opened his chest panel.

"Oh. That's probably not good, is it?" said Mr Finn.

"He's been around for over two hundred years," said Megan. "He's very resilient."

"Yes. My robots are too."

"Kevin, could you gag Mr Finn or something? Just with anything you can find. Rope, socks, fish... whatever."

Happy to be of further use, Kevin forced some of the remaining rope into Mr Finn's mouth.

Megan could see that all TJ's wires and cables were still there; they were just a bit damp. She reconnected her Goozberri Five, once again bypassing Mr Finn's chip.

Everything was reconnected. All the water had been emptied out of his head. Nothing.

"Of course," said Megan, pressing the button on TJ's neck. "Reboot!"

There was some fizzing and sparking from inside TJ, but his eyes flickered to life again, back to his familiar flashing blue.

"Megan," said TJ. "Oh no, Megan…"

"I know TJ, you couldn't help it. It's ok."

"No. Megan. Look out." TJ pointed upwards. Phoenix was hovering above them, ready to swoop down and strike.

# CHAPTER 45...

# SINK AND SWIM

Megan flew upwards without thinking, smashing into the side of the huge metal bird. It pushed down, gripping her with its talons and swooping low, forcing her towards the river and under the water. Spluttering, Megan twisted around so she was facing away from Phoenix, then used its strength to propel herself upwards and over the top of the robot in an arc.

*Hey*, thought Megan, *finally got that loop the loop right*.

John watched from the dockside. He could see Megan dodging and weaving in the sky, trying to evade Phoenix. He could also see that around their little dinghy, the river had started to glow. He kept trying to change, but he was too weak. Suddenly, there was a rumble from the sheds. John turned, fearing the worst. Sure enough, there was Evolve, rolling slowly towards him.

256

Beneath the river, unaware of the trouble above, seal-Cam had led Lily back down to the shield. Lily spotted the four sigil coins and removed them, but the gate remained open. They would need Jimmy and all the sigils in place to lock it again. She put them back in their slots and pointed upwards so seal-Cam could understand he needed to fetch TJ.

Cam was starting to think it was nearly all finished when Resilience reappeared out of the dark water behind Lily and grabbed her arm.

Meanwhile, back on the dinghy, Kevin realised it was his turn to be a hero.

"How can we help?" said TJ.

"I've got an idea," he told TJ. "Mr Finn said you were on the same frequency as his robots, right?"

Mr Finn glared at Kevin, which made Kevin even more sure he was on the right track.

"That is correct," said TJ.

"So… is there a way we could send a signal to help you control them?"

"It is possible to transmit the control signal using my Morse-code machine," said TJ. "Then I would control the sculptures."

257

"Excellent! What's the signal?"

"U. R. V." said TJ. "Dot dot dash. Dot dash dot. Dot dot dot dash."

Kevin tapped out the signal.

"Now issue this command," said TJ. "Dash dash dash. Dot dot dash dot. Dot dot dash dot."

"What's that?" said Kevin, tapping the signal out.

"Off." said TJ.

Under the water, the lights went out in Resilience's eyes and he let go of Lily.

On the dockside, Evolve's slow rumble towards John abruptly ceased.

And in the sky above, Phoenix stopped, and plunged down to the river, dragging Megan with it as it fell.

TJ immediately dived in after her.

Megan had never really liked the water. Even though she had learned to swim well, she never enjoyed it. And now that she was so used to spinning and twirling in the air, being underwater made her feel much heavier than it ever had before. Although, to be fair, the fact that she was tangled up in a huge metal sculpture probably wasn't helping.

Below, she could make out the two dark shapes of seal-Cam and Lily, silhouetted against the green glow. She was sinking fast, looking down upon it all like one of those dreams where you are falling. With a slow bump, the statue settled at the bottom of the river.

At once, Cam and Lily were beside her, trying to pull her free from Phoenix. Megan was still holding her breath, but she knew if they couldn't loosen Phoenix's grip soon, she would be in serious trouble. So she was delighted to see TJ landing on the riverbed beside them. He pulled at the statue too, bending back the wings until Megan was free.

Lily grabbed her and began swimming quickly up to the surface. Even as they sped upwards, time seemed to slow down. Megan saw TJ place his hand on the shield's panel, turning it first right then left, and the gap in the riverbed slowly began to close. She caught one quick glimpse of strange moving colours within – what looked like electrical and chemical lights flickering into life – and then the shield was shut.

# CHAPTER 46...

## HELLO AND CHEERIO

Kevin had rowed back over to the dock and was sitting beside John when the others finally emerged from the river. Mr Finn sat scowling in the dinghy.

"Did you do it?" said John, wincing as he stood up. "Is it locked?"

"The power under the river is safe," said TJ. "We need only hide the sigils once again."

"Brilliant!" said John. "I knew you could do it."

"What is it we did exactly?" asked Lily.

Megan smiled. "Sorry Lily, you must think we're all really rude. We'd only just met and I was ordering you to dive under the river with a total stranger and fight giant robots."

"Well, it's certainly one way to get to know new people," said Lily.

"That's a good point," said Megan, "proper introductions. You know Cam and me, that's Kevin in the dinghy, the robot is called Tin Jimmy, but we all call him TJ, and this is John. He's sort of a retired guardian, and our coach!"

"Hello." Lily smiled and gave an embarrassed wave.

"And I'm Mr Finn," said Mr Finn through the rope in his mouth.

"Ignore him," said Cam, "he's the baddie."

"And he's in big trouble," said Kevin. "It seems that *someone* has tipped off the police about all the strange weapons in his house and the mess his sculptures have made. They're on their way."

Mr Finn glared at Kevin.

"And when I say 'someone', I mean ME," beamed Kevin.

"Yeah Kev, we got that," said Cam.

Megan sat down next to Lily, who was still looking a bit confused.

"So Lily, I'm guessing you've figured out that we all have something in common?" asked Megan.

"Yes," said Lily, "but I don't know what you mean by 'guardian'. I saw you a few times before, at the dam and the river... and I wanted to say hello but... today I just knew I had to come here."

"Was there a fizzing in your chest?" asked Kevin. "Like too much sherbet and curry powder mixed together?"

"That's it! What does it mean? Why do we have superpowers?"

John smiled. "You all have a lot of catching up to do," he said. He began limping towards the warehouse door.

"We need to get you to a hospital first, John," said Megan.

"Rubbish," he said. "Wind on my face, grass underfoot and I'll be fine." He turned and winked at Cam. "This guy knows what I mean." John then hobbled back to Megan and gave her a little hug. "Thanks for rescuing me," he said.

"We all did it together!" said Megan.

"No, I mean before. When I was hiding in a cave." He quickly turned his attentions to the robot. "Jimmy! It was great to work with you again. I think it's fair to say you've aged better than me."

"There have been many replacement parts," said TJ.

John nodded and smiled. "Kevin, Lily, stick in with this lot, they'll see you right. Help me to the road Cam, would you? I think I'm feeling well enough to change and head home for a rest now."

Cam walked slowly with John, out into the unusual sun of a spring day. The river sparkled, and the green of the hills shimmered in the heat.

"Do you remember when we were wolves, Cam?"

"Course I do. It was amazing."

"Exactly. But you can have too much of a good thing," said John. "Two feet on the ground, mind."

"I know," said Cam. "I won't forget."

Cam watched the black cat pad gently out of the docks, heading for the wide-open spaces.

CHAPTER 47...

# BEGINNINGS AND ENDINGS

"I still can't believe we did it," said Megan quietly, the enormity of the day before finally catching up with her. "We really did it..." She jumped up and hugged a surprised Cam, lifting him slightly off the ground, then she ran and kissed TJ on his tin cheek.

They had brought the new guardians to John's cave, but John was nowhere to be seen.

"Yeah, it was amazing!" said Kevin, slightly fading away with excitement. "What should we do next? Let's make some plans!"

"Chippy? I'm starving," said Cam.

"We should have a team name," said Kevin, "like Awesome Patrol or Mega-Amazing Force! I could draw us a logo."

Megan laughed. "I do feel pretty mega-amazing."

"I also think codenames would be cool," said Kevin.

263

"I said that ages ago Kev, but we decided not to bother," said Cam.

"No, I think you were right," said Megan. "We can't keep shouting our own names at one another during fights with supervillains, can we?"

"Brilliant!" said Kevin, taking a folded-up bit of paper out of his pocket. "I've got some suggestions. For you Megan, how about Velocity Girl! Or Sparrowhawk!"

"Sparrowhawk?" said Cam. "That's rubbish."

"I've already thought of mine," said Megan, thinking of her gran. "I'm Kite." Megan put on her best serious superhero face and floated up into the air with her hands on her hips, "Kite, scourge of the skies."

"You sure you don't mean 'Balloon, full of hot air'?" said Cam. "What's mine then Kev?"

"I was thinking you could be Metamorpho! Or Wereboy!"

Megan snorted. "Definitely Wereboy. Very cute. Sounds like a cuddly toy."

"Cameron could be called The Amazing Hamster Boy," said TJ. "Or perhaps just Hamster Boy."

"I'd prefer Kid Kong," said Cam.

"You change into all sorts of things though," said Megan.

"Yeah but gorilla's the coolest one."

"Just now," said Megan, "but you might find cooler things to turn into."

"Like a jellyfish perhaps," said TJ, "or a sloth."

"This is actually quite tricky, isn't it?" said Cam, ignoring TJ and thinking hard. "Cam-eleon?" Cam growled and did his superhero pose, "*Cam*-eleon, king of the jungle."

"Lions are King of the jungle," said TJ, "chameleons are tiny lizards."

"Ok, the catchphrase needs work, but the name's staying."

"What about you, Kevin?" said Megan.

"Wraith!" said Kevin.

"That's a bad-guy name," said Cam. "He'd be like your invisible arch-enemy."

"Shadow!"

"Goodies aren't called Shadow," said Cam, "unless they are dogs or horses."

"Ghost!" Kevin had clearly put a lot of thought into this.

"Ghost. Yeah," said Megan. "Ghost sounds pretty cool."

"Yeah, I've got my catchphrase too," said Kevin, fading away completely. "Ghost – he's behind you!"

"Now you sound like a panto villain," said Cam, shuddering, because he actually was quite scared of panto.

"Kite, Chameleon, Ghost and … what about you Lily?"

Lily had been sitting biting her nails and smiling as the rest of them talked.

"Oh. I don't want a name."

"Course you do!" said Kevin. "I'm sure I could think of something good..."

Lily shook her head. "No, its ok."

"Come on Lily," said Megan. "Your power is incredible. I sank like a stone down there and you were all whirlpools and bubbles."

"Really?" said Lily.

"Really," said Cam. "You totally saved me and John."

"Right Kev, let's hear some ideas," said Megan.

"She-Kraken!"

Lily wrinkled her nose. "Uhm..."

"Atlantia!"

"Right..."

"Siren!"

"Another baddie," said Cam, exasperated. "You haven't joined this team by mistake when you meant to join up with the League of Evil or something?"

Kevin wasn't even listening. "Sprite!"

"I like Sprite," said Lily quickly.

"Yeah, I think that would totally suit you," said Megan. "Excellent. Kevin, homework for tomorrow is team names and logos. Then I suppose we can think about masks."

"Right now," said Cam, "I'd be more interested in hot chocolate and biscuits. I don't think I'll ever feel warm after being in the river yesterday."

Lily nodded. "Hot chocolate would be nice."

"I will put the kettle on," said TJ.

Megan watched as her robot trundled over to John's makeshift kitchen. She was sure she heard him say, "There are five."

Her mind instantly turned to her gran again. It had taken a while, but she had managed to do what Gran had wanted: protect the town and the river with the help of her friends. The fizzing in her stomach felt a little different now: stronger, but warmer too. Yesterday, she had been exhausted; now she felt as if she could fly higher than the sun. She turned to look at Cam, and noticed that he had his hand on his chest. He nodded at her and smiled.

"So... not that I'm complaining... but does anyone want to tell me and Lily where the superpowers come from?" asked Kevin. "I'm not sure I can wait any longer."

Megan smiled. "Sorry Kev." She turned round to face them all properly. "I'll tell it to you as it was told to me. Almost three hundred years ago, not long after the very start of our little town, there was a storm..."

THE
GREENOCK
GAZETTE 50p

# JAIL BREAK!!!

Disgraced Waterworx CEO Egon Finn has shocked prison staff with his 'inexplicable' disappearance from his cell last night.

Only a few weeks ago, Finn was imprisoned for designing and manufacturing enormous violent robots disguised as public art sculptures, which attacked citizens and knocked down listed historic buildings. A search of his house later revealed a huge underground laboratory filled with dangerous weapons and plans for world domination.

He was also being held under suspicion of poisoning the water and causing the recent surge of mutated fish washing up on the shores of the Clyde. Prison guards arrived at his cell this morning to discover a huge hole melted in the wall. Despite his cell being more than one hundred feet above the ground, it is assumed Finn escaped through the hole.

The public are warned not to approach Finn. He should be considered very dangerous and potentially diabolical.